I0534108

Vlora

Rafael Avtino

Copyright © 2013 by Rafael Avtino.

All rights reserved. No part of this publication may be reproduced, stored in a retrieval system or transmitted, in any form, or by any means, electronic, mechanical, recorded, photocopied, or otherwise, without the prior permission of the copyright owner.

Published by Amethyst Sky Publishing.

Cover Design by Anu Design.

Manufactured in The United States of America.

ISBN: 978-0-578-13394-2

Table of Contents

How terrifying the mind can be.

Chapter 1

Lightning stretched across the night sky like complicated thoughts do the mind. Thunder bellowed to the extreme. As rain hammered down, torrential streams of water gushed through the streets of the little neighborhood. Wind raced over the roofs of all the houses like it was trying to escape from a predator's grasp. The sky resembled a veiled executioner.

Vlora gazed through her bedroom window at the storm outside. Her expression was like that of a grieving widow. In her white night gown, she looked almost like a ghost. She sighed. Walked away from the window. Picked up her hair brush. As she ran the brush through her hair, she looked emptily at the mirror in front of her.

She opened an empty drawer, placed the brush inside, closed the drawer, and walked away. That drawer, however, was certainly capable of holding much more than just an innocent brush.

Chapter 2

Vlora Whitaker was a strong woman. Even though she hardly ever smiled or laughed, she always gave herself much credit for helping others and showing respect. This inner sense of purpose kept her going through each day. Still, she was very lonely. Every night she pondered over past childhood crushes, adolescent romances, and college date failures. She never felt that the men she met were good enough for her.

She took great pride in her appearance, believing she could even become a model—but she did not care for that career path. Her hair had always been naturally wavy, and it never took much brushing up to look absolutely stunning. It was the darkest black—as black as her nightmares, in fact. Her skin was rather pale, though sometimes she got tans and came out with a peachy skin tone. She loved how flawless her skin was. It seemed like it was dipped every morning in a river of milk and honey. Her lipstick was always of the latest style. She made sure to read all the latest fashion magazines, and constantly tried to imitate the looks within. However, she always went for the dark looks. This meant her dresses were usually black, as well as her boots. Sometimes she would wear scarves of another color, usually worn when the weather was not even cold.

One morning, she parked her car in a downtown parking lot and walked to her job at an office building. A typical workday morning. Cars whizzed by, honking ensued, the sound of nearby construction blared, people criss-crossed through the streets, traffic signals changed non-stop, a hobo wandered aimlessly around and asked people for money, and throngs of businesspeople trying to get to work walked along the sidewalks. The energy she experienced as she walked on contrasted deeply with her home's silence. She felt almost shocked going to and from work every day, as the volume levels around the workplace and within her home were so different. In her home, she sometimes felt like she was lost within the far reaches of outer space. Here in downtown, however, she sometimes believed she was being suffocated.

She walked into her office building. It was glass-windowed, modern, and sturdy. She worked as a businesswoman and loved her job. She was not the most social person in the workplace, but she had friends who worked with her. Somehow, dealing with financial matters made her feel more confident. She enjoyed helping people with financial challenges while learning about her clients' personalities.

"Morning, Ms. Whitaker!"

She was so focused on getting to her cubicle on time, for a few moments she was not able to discern who gave her this greeting. She finally noticed it was Mr. Morford, a receptionist who worked on the first floor.

"Good morning, Mr. Morford. Nice morning, isn't it?" she responded.

"It is, it is!" Mr. Morford smiled. "And another great day for you to keep practicing that communication!" he laughed.

She laughed as well, but thought to herself, *what an asshole*. She took an elevator to the eighth floor, where she worked. When she arrived at her cubicle, she noticed she was a few minutes late, but figured she might as well work a few extra minutes anyway. She sifted through papers left on her desk from the previous workday and realized there was much work to do. Although she enjoyed doing such work, she knew how exhausting it could be. Little did she know, this day's work would be so exhausting, she would have a hard time not falling asleep by the time she finished it.

****

When all the day's work was complete, Vlora sighed, got up from her cubicle, and began to walk to the elevator. One of her friends and co-workers, Mrs. Clark, stopped her on the way. Mrs. Clark was a caring, funny, and supportive woman. She was African-American and physically very strong. Vlora always thought she lifted weights at the gym, but she denied it, sometimes saying "the gym is for wusses".

Mrs. Clark glanced at her with raised eyebrows and asked "are you all right? You don't look so well today."

Vlora chuckled. "Well, it was just very busy today. You know how those days roll."

"Oh yeah, honey. I know all right. Are you in a rush, by any chance?"

"Oh, no! Not at all. Did you need to tell me something?"

"Yes. And I'm not kidding what I'm about to say. Sweetie, lately you've been looking kind of down, and I have to ask…have you gone out with anyone recently?"

Vlora was shocked. "No, why do you ask?"

"Vlora. You're forty years old and still single. You haven't had a boyfriend since college. I think it's about time…"

"For me to get a boyfriend?" Vlora asked and then laughed.

"Well, why not?" Mrs. Clark shook her head. "I think a good man could get you smiling more often and feeling extra special." She paused and looked around to make sure no one was watching them. "I'm afraid to say it, Vlora, but you're really a shy one. I think it's time you started to open up a little more…let loose every now and then. It's not good to be so serious and locked up inside yourself all the time."

Vlora understood. She knew Mrs. Clark was right, but was just afraid to admit it.

Mrs. Clark calmly laid her hand on Vlora's shoulder, discreetly pointed at a male co-worker, and asked "see that man there? The guy with blond hair?"

Vlora looked at where she pointed and made out a good-looking blond man who appeared about her own age. The office in which she worked was large, with over forty employees all bunched up in cubicles, and she had never met the man or known his name. But of course she saw him there all the time, and always thought he was very handsome.

"Yes, I see him."

"Well, his name is Pete. He is the sweetest guy…and I know I'm married and all, but damn, if I weren't, you better believe I'd be all over him. The guy's single and, at least from what I know, in serious need of some friends. Vlora, he may be the one for you."

"I'm sorry…but how do you know him?"

"Oh, he's delivered some work to me here in the office, and occasionally we'll sit and talk for a few seconds. And I have to say again, he's the sweetest guy. Honey, why don't you ask him out to dinner some time? I'm sure he'd love it!"

She grimaced at the thought, and then shook her head. "You're kidding me, right? Jenny, you know how shy I am! And that guy's hot; I'd probably melt in a little puddle right in front of him."

Laughing, Mrs. Clark told her "I know you're shy! But honey, you've just got to start getting out there! Life doesn't wait. I think it's time now for you to just…do it!"

She looked again at Pete. He was sifting through some files, occasionally wrinkling his forehead. But oh, how handsome he was! She blushed and looked at Mrs. Clark with a slight smile. "Oh, all right."

"Now that's a girl! Hah!" Mrs. Clark playfully slapped her on the shoulder. "I am so proud of you. You've got guts, that's my girl."

As Vlora neared the elevator, she thought to herself, *I can't believe the shit I'm getting into. But will it really be that bad? It might be something very good, actually.* She got into the elevator and smiled. *Something new, for a change.*

****

The next morning, Vlora made sure to groom herself extra carefully. She inspected her entire black dress for unusual markings, found none, and moved on to other items she would wear. Despite her initial misgivings, she sprayed loads of perfume on herself. Her lipstick had to look perfect. She brushed her hair with the precision of a good doctor performing surgery.

She practiced walking confidently as she marched to work, and welcomed every look of admiration on the sidewalk. Certainly, she looked like a model striding down the runway in only the finest elegance. Black elegance. As she entered her office building, she glided swiftly past Mr. Morford and ignored anything the bastard could have said to her. She had to have a clear and confident mind in preparation for speaking with this…Pete.

Unlike the previous day, this was a quick workday. When she completed her work, she glanced over at Pete to see if he was done as well. *Oh! He is. How cute.* She walked steadily, trying not to stumble, over to his cubicle. *Please don't make a fool of yourself, Vlora. The last thing I need today is a complete disaster. Just be strong, like you know you can be.* As she arrived, Pete looked slowly up at her.

"Hi! You're Pete, right?"

Pete paused, and then replied "yes ma'am! You're…"

"Vlora Whitaker. I work three rows down."

"Oh, yes. I've seen you at your cubicle sometimes. You're a very hard worker."

"Hah!" she fake-laughed. "I tend to work hard sometimes. My friend Jenny, over there, told me you were very knowledgeable." *I'm going too damn fast.*

"Oh, yeah. Jenny Clark. She thinks everybody's an expert, though."

No! Now what do I say? "Well, she seemed pretty adamant about you, though. You know, the world needs smarter people." She felt like she messed up with the 'smart' comments. "So anyway, what do you do?"

"I'm an accountant for clients on the far northeast side of the city. Just people with small businesses who'd like to keep their accounts safe. Yeah, it's a pretty…menial job, to say the least," Pete chuckled.

"Oh, that actually sounds really cool. I'm sure you're quite good with numbers," she fake-laughed again.

"Well yeah, I have to be. So is your shift already done?"

"Very much so, very much so. Is yours?"

"Yes, actually."

"Are you…busy this evening?"

Pete's shoulders slightly hunched up. "No, actually, I'm not. Why?"

"Well, I was just thinking…how does dinner tonight sound?"

"I think it sounds great. Dinner with who, though?"

She believed sweat was forming on her forehead. "I was thinking just me and you. We can discuss business matters."

Pete stared blankly for a few seconds. "That sounds great!"

"Great!" she blurted out. "And I'm sorry, but I didn't get your whole name. Pete…"

"Harrington."

"And is it just Pete, or Peter?"

"It's just plain old Pete," he said, laughing.

"Is Carrie's Café across the street at six p.m. all right?"

"Oh yes, I love that place!"

"Wonderful!" She half-sighed with relief. "Well it was

very nice meeting you, Pete."

"Likewise, Ms. Whitaker."

"And I'll see you there!"

"See ya!"

She walked away, trying hard not to blush. *He is so hot...and I'm having dinner with him tonight! How wonderful!* She could not help but smile as she walked across the eighth floor to the elevator. *But what am I going to do for a whole hour?* She had an hour until dinner, and did not know how to pass that time. *Oh well.* She decided on pretending to do work at a coffee shop across the street.

Fifteen minutes before six p.m., she gulped and began to tremble. Even though she had sifted through her files during the past forty-five minutes in the coffee shop, trying to think of what to talk about with Pete, she felt like there were simply not enough work-related issues to talk about. And although this left room for her and Pete to get to more personal matters, which was what she wanted anyway, she was not sure whether Pete would be so willing to discuss such issues. He seemed unusually stiff when she introduced herself. This did not bode well for the possibility of a normal and spontaneous conversation.

Carrie's Café. The time had come. Vlora sat at a bar with her chin in her palm, waiting for Pete. She had ordered herself a coke, but was not sure what drink Pete would like. Finally, he arrived. He smiled when he saw her sitting so quietly at the bar. She did not even notice him as he plunked down in the seat next to her.

"Why hello, Ms. Whitaker!" he declared.

She was startled at first, but then quickly relaxed. "Oh, you can call me Vlora. And do you go by Pete or Mr. Harrington?"

"You can call me Pete. Plain and simple, hah."

"Yeah, let's just keep it that way."

Pete ordered a beer and continually smiled as he and

Vlora talked away on business matters. Vlora was amazed at Pete's knowledge. *This guy really knows what he's talking about*. After about thirty minutes, though, she felt like they were running out of work-related topics. They both began to fidget. Pete initiated the next conversation.

"So, have you seen any good movies lately?"

Vlora was a little stunned, but inside she cheered loudly. "Well…um, no, actually. Have you?"

Pete smiled and said "it's good to know that I'm not alone! Seems like there's nothing good out right now. So what did you do this past weekend?"

"Me? I…uh…went grocery shopping, read some books, went to the mall for a bit. Yeah, that's just about it. You?"

"I also went grocery shopping! How 'bout that? My brother came to visit from Cincinnati. We hung out together a lot. You know, sometimes I'm amazed by him. He's a psychiatrist, and any little mood swing I have, he'll tell me what's wrong with me, try to fix it, and I swear to God, it works all the time!" he laughed.

Oh my goodness gracious. Vlora fake-smiled. *Well, it's okay to get mood swings. That's completely natural, right?* "Oh, I wish I had a brother like that. I mean, I have a brother, but he's not an expert in…well, you know, mental issues."

Pete's eyes widened. "So you do have a brother. That's nice. Any sisters?"

"Nope. It's just my one brother. What about you? Do you have any other siblings?"

"I actually have two other brothers, older, and no sisters. So we were a very...you know, rowdy type of bunch."

"Oh, I understand."

"Yeah, there was always lots of competition around the household."

"I understand that too. Even me and my brother, growing up, we were so competitive. I think I proved myself stronger than him the majority of the time."

Pete laughed at this. "You do look like a very tough woman."

"Yeah, I certainly showed him," she also laughed.

"Are you married?"

She was astonished that he would ask this so quickly. *But maybe it isn't too soon.* "No. I'm very single." She wondered whether she should ask the dreaded corresponding question. *Oh yes I will. Suck it up and take a chance.* "How 'bout you, are you married?"

"No. I've never been married, actually."

Her heart screamed with joy. "Well...I find that surprising. You seem like a very nice guy."

"Mmm...I can be."

What else would you be, Mr. Pete? She did not know what else to say, and had had enough awkwardness for one day. "Well it was nice speaking with you here. You are very smart. I'll definitely be taking your advice."

"It was a nice dinner indeed, and I hope we can meet like this more often; I think meetings like this are a big help. And keep working as hard as you do. I think you're my new role model."

Jenny was right. He is a sweetheart. "Bye, Pete. I'll see you Monday."

"See you, Vlora!"

She walked briskly out of the café. *Too much conversation. Way too much conversation. But I absolutely love it.*

Chapter 3

Vlora arrived home laughing. *I did it! I actually met an extremely hot guy! Oh, how wonderful!* Her bliss was like a stroll through a sunny park after months of rain. She danced and sang while doing her nightly chores, feeling as if she were not working at all.

After cleaning her kitchen counter, she plopped down in the living room couch to watch some T.V.. *Just the usual crime and violence on today. Give me a break.*

When it was ten p.m., she became exhausted. She glanced at the grandfather clock next to the T.V., and it started to blur. Such blurs usually happened whenever she became tired. She was completely used to it. She put on her night gown and brushed her hair, her usual nightly routine. *I am so beautiful. How can any man not want me?*

After using the bathroom, she turned on the lamp which stood on her nightstand and turned off all the other lights. She needed at least one light on every night, and this lamp did the trick. She did not like complete darkness—at all. As she lay down on her bed, she thought of her lonely life.

Already forty years old, and not one boyfriend since college. So wrong. Oh, Vlora. How dare you stay single for so long. Life is more than a fun job and a clean house. Not even a dog around here. Damn. My life...why is it so screwed up? Everything is so horrible when I'm by myself! I'm messed up! Swarming throughout my head, all these thoughts. They're like a demon to me. My mind is my enemy, I swear to God. Get me away from it. Get me away from it! Too many people...everywhere. But I have to meet more. I'm so complicated. Everything is complicated. This house is complicated...right? I hope not. Stupid cleanliness...for what? No one comes here! Ever! I can invite Jenny. She's so nice to me. I gotta be nicer to her; I haven't done anything for her. Have I actually done anything for anybody? Probably not. Well, what a shame. How can someone so afraid of people...meet more people? I know I have to meet more. Will my mind allow me to? The goddamn mind. Always screwed up. It is the only thing that can prevent me from meeting more people.

And she lay there, with her eyes wide open. They were wide open.

She glanced at the wall opposite her bed. *Such a clean wall.* Not for long. Five black dots spanning the length of a hand suddenly appeared on it. They slowly extended downwards, becoming lines that kept reaching downwards. Finally, the lines stopped stretching about two feet from the floor. They had been placed upon the wall as if someone with unusually sharp finger nails had scraped them downwards along it. Except, there was no one standing in front of the wall. *Is the wall peeling? There has to be some logical explanation for this.*

There was a wall to the right of the bedroom's door. This wall stood next to Vlora's bed. A shadow of a hand swiftly grasped the edge of the wall from outside the door. It stayed there holding onto the wall for several seconds, it seemed. No details of the hand were visible, because the light from the lamp was not strong enough where the hand was.

Vlora tried to move her body, but found she could not. She was stuck in the same position she had been in while pondering her loneliness. *What is happening to me? What has come over my body? Oh, I'm going to die tonight! Someone is going to kill me!*

Immediately, the shadow of the person whose hand was on the wall walked completely into the room. It stopped right in front of Vlora's bed. She had never been so terrified. While the shadow was there, it seemed to be staring at her. It stayed there for a few seconds and then began to walk even closer to her. In the light of the lamp, she could see the shadow more clearly. It was a person covered in a black robe and hood. This person looked almost exactly like images of the Grim Reaper which she had seen before. The only differences were that this person did not hold a scythe, and no face was visible. Where there would be a face, she could only make out a black veil covering the shape of a face.

The intruder slowly walked nearer to her. Unable to move at all, she stared helplessly at it, with her eyes wide open. *Please don't kill me, person from Hell.* Sweat began to form on her forehead. Her hand was the first part of her body to show signs of movement. It started to twitch uncontrollably. Her heart beat faster and faster.

Soon, the intruder was standing right next to her. Glancing up, she noticed that it was strangely calm in its demeanor. It seemed almost arrogant, in fact. *It knows things I don't know. It has a power over me I cannot control.*

The intruder bent over her, staring at her through its dark veil. She tried to move her entire body with the most determination she ever had. This was impossible at first, but she did not want to die so helpless. Instantly, she screamed as loud as a train horn. She sat up in her bed, close to sobbing.

The intruder was gone. She looked around her room with astonishment. Surprisingly, the room looked exactly the same as it did when she first laid herself down on the bed. The walls were clean again.

"Where the hell are you?" she asked the emptiness.

No reply.

"I'm not afraid of you!" she lied.

The room was so quiet, she thought she could hear her own heartbeat. *It is my own heartbeat, right?* Terrified, she grasped herself like a little child. *What the hell just happened?* She wondered if the person she had just seen was hiding in her closet. *I must defend myself.*

Slowly, she got up from her bed and walked across the room to her closet. There was no one inside. She investigated her entire room for signs of intrusion. Nothing. *This is impossible. I saw the damn person with my own eyes. They were open. Absolutely open!* She felt the wall which, just a while before, had five mysterious lines on it. There were no longer any suspicious markings or indentations in it. Trembling, she walked outside her room and scoured the entire house for signs of disturbance. Everything looked completely normal.

I am not crazy. I saw someone…in my room. There was someone who wanted to kill me…in my room. I am not psychotic. My eyes were open! I wasn't even asleep! Was it a ghost? No, of course not. Don't be unreasonable, Vlora. Everything has a logical explanation. But ghosts are logical, right? They can be. No one has proven their existence, but that doesn't mean they don't exist. How weird. I could have seen a ghost. I have to tell Jenny about this. Or Nathan. They'll laugh at me. No, not Nathan. He's so understanding…sometimes. I'm exhausted. Simply exhausted. Screw anyone else in this house, I'm gonna sleep right now.

But sleep did not come that easy.

****

When Vlora woke up, she was relieved it was daytime. *No more ghosts of the night, thank goodness.* She made herself a filling breakfast, dressed nicely, and sat herself down at the computer. She wanted to research possible reasons for the past night's nightmarish episode.

After a few minutes of desperate research, she gasped.

"Hypnagogic hallucinations. So that's what they are." *At*

least it wasn't a ghost. I knew reason would overcome.
"Hypnagogia, the word from which 'hypnagogic' is derived,
describes the state between being awake and falling asleep."
Yeah, that's definitely the state I was in. "The sensations
experienced while hallucinating in the hypnagogic state may be
visual, auditory, and tactile. Hypnagogic hallucinations may be
accompanied by sleep paralysis." *That's why I had so much
trouble moving.* "During sleep paralysis, the person may feel like
he or she is being pressed down, imagine the presence of
someone, and feel an intense fear." *That describes my experience
perfectly.* "The eyes of the person experiencing the
hallucinations may be open the whole time."

That last description made her shiver. She knew her eyes
were open during the episode. And even though it was
completely normal for eyes to be open while hallucinating, she
felt weak realizing that she had actually seen, with her own eyes,
someone walking through her room. This made her mind seem
so much more vulnerable. *I can't believe my mind can lead me
astray like that.*

All of a sudden, her doorbell rang. She jumped in her
seat. *I haven't invited anyone. Who can that be?* She got up and
walked slowly to the front door. *I must be brave.* She stood for a
few moments in front of the door, wondering whether she should
have looked through her window first. *Don't be pathetic.*

It was her older brother, Nathan. He was very handsome,
with black hair and dark brown eyes. Like Vlora, he was a little
bit on the shy side. However, he had always been a good brother,
and whenever Vlora needed some advice, he was the first to be
there for her.

"Nathan! How good to see you."

"Nice to see you, too! It's been a while, eh? Almost a
month, I would say."

"Well, I'm sorry about that." She knew it was her fault.
Within the past month, Nathan had often asked her if he could

come to visit, but she always refused his offer on the basis of being too busy. She was hardly busy at all.

"No, no. Don't go blaming yourself. I know how busy you are. You're a hard worker, Vlora."

"Eh…"

"You are, and don't ever change that. That's one of the reasons I respect you so much. I just came to say hi and see how things are going for you." Nathan noticed her computer was out. "You've been working on the computer?"

Her heart jumped. She also realized she had not closed any of the internet tabs. "Oh, yes! Just…doing a little research, that's all."

"On what?"

Leave me alone, Nathan. "On…on…"

His eyes widened.

"Nathan. I have something I need to tell you." She felt ashamed. "Last night…something weird happened to me. I was going to bed as usual, and…I was very tired, and…I saw some very scary things. I thought I saw someone else walking around my room." She paused, and then continued. "So this morning I wanted to do research on why I experienced this strange vision. As it turns out, there are these things called hypnagogic hallucinations. They're terrifying. Sometimes you don't know if what you're seeing is imagined…or real."

Nathan shook his head. "Vlora…I hope you're all right. Is everything all right?"

"Oh, yes! Don't get me wrong. I'm a very tough woman, I've already overcome the fear from that stupid hallucination. I'm perfectly all right."

After a few awkward seconds, Nathan gulped and said "I'm your big brother, Vlora. I want you to know that I'll be there for you, anytime you feel scared or anything like that. Just give me a call! I don't know why you didn't after that experience; I know I would have been scared as hell. Are you sure you're doing all right?"

Now she was getting somewhat irritated. "Yes, Nathan! What, you don't trust me?"

He gave her a wistful look, and after a while said "yes. Of course I do."

"Well then." She tried to think of a new subject, and came up with something actually not too far from the same subject. "Nathan. You remember when I was a little girl, right?"

"Yes. Why?"

"Well, back then, I used to be fascinated by the dark and gloomy. I used to daydream about such things…"

With closed eyes, she remembered one of these daydreams. She was a little girl now, about twelve years old, in a cute little dress. She found herself in a large, weed-filled front yard. It was nighttime. The front yard belonged to a Victorian style, wooden, and three-story house. She looked innocently up at this house. It seemed to stare back at her as lightning flashed across the sky behind it. A light was on behind one of the windows below the attic. *Who could live inside such a dreary house?* She turned around. There in front of her stood a horrifying witch. The witch had a pointed hat, deathly skin, a crooked nose, a black cloak, wrinkled boots, and a gaze of absolute murder. She screamed and ran away from the witch, out of the front gate, and through a dark road. She saw a black cat run across the road in front of her. As the cat was running, it looked back at her, and she noticed its eyes were an evil red.

Forty years old again, she opened her eyes and looked straight at Nathan. "I was strange, wasn't I?"

Nathan lowered the corners of his mouth. "I remember you were always a little…different. Not that there's anything wrong with that, you know."

"Different?" She laughed. "I was awesome!"

"Yes, you were!" Nathan laughed as well.

She calmed down after a while, and began a completely

different conversation. "So, how's Linda doing?"

"She's doing great! She just bought herself a new garden statue, one that has two little children playing together with a bucket and a shovel. It's cute; I like it."

"Well isn't that sweet? She's always such a sweetie."

Nathan nodded his head. "You know, I have to ask you, Vlora...has anyone come into your life lately? I think it's about time."

Shut up, shut up, shut up. "You know...no. No one yet."

After a pause, he said "it's okay if someone does, you know. Sometimes you just have to be a little more inviting."

She gave him an icy stare.

"But if you're happy, Vlora...well, that's all that matters."

Oh, Nathan. I love you so. "Thanks."

They continued to talk together for some time, and when Nathan said goodbye and left the house, Vlora smiled to herself. *Nathan. A man I can count on.*

****

Nighttime came again. Vlora had spent her day grocery shopping and reading romance novels. The usual. She was now watching T.V. and exercising in her living room. Her exercise was based on what she was watching, and she tried her hardest to imitate the moves performed by the woman on screen. *Damn you, lady. You make it look so easy.*

By the time all the exercise was done, she was exhausted. And it was only eight p.m.. She realized she had not had dinner yet. *Spaghetti sounds delicious. I'll go ahead and make that.* Her dinners were almost always spent by herself. She never felt a great urge to invite others over, and hardly ever went out to social gatherings. Her reserve, and fear of the unknown, screamed to her to avoid such things as much as possible.

Sometimes, however, she would daydream about putting on skin-tight clothing, plastering her face in makeup, and exploring the alleyways of the city. There were bound to be many dance clubs, just waiting for her to become the Queen of the Night. Maybe she would find a young man, too. And then she could prostitute herself...over and over again. The heavy breathing, the screams of pleasure, the refreshing warmth of a real man!

But these were just daydreams.

Silence. So much of it, in fact, that she decided to turn the T.V. back on. She flipped past all the channels which had violence. There were quite a few. She finally found a nice game show to watch. *Now this is what I'm talking about. Funny and entertaining.*

She heard a scraping sound against the roof. It sounded almost like someone with unusually sharp finger nails scraping them along it. She felt a chill run down her spine. *Scraping. That's happened before here. Just one night ago, actually.* She slowly looked up. Everything looked completely normal. She muted the T.V., and after a few seconds, again heard the same scraping sound. *An animal. That's all it is. Some silly little raccoon, trying to scare me. Pathetic.* She put the volume back on.

After the game show ended, she stretched, double checked the roof, found nothing wrong, and walked into her bedroom. She did not even notice that her window shutters were wide open. All she wanted to do was check to make sure that her files were in order. *Everything has to be where it should be. Work has been getting busier than usual, and I don't want to be sitting in the office Monday with a headache from messed up files.* So she began to diligently organize her files.

Outside, in the night, a person covered in a black robe and hood slowly crept towards Vlora's bedroom window. The shutters were open, all right. This person had no trouble watching her organize everything through the open shutters.

When Vlora was done with her files, she sighed, looked at

the time, and decided to make herself a late night snack. *A nice sandwich would hit the spot.* She walked to her kitchen, ate with infatuation, and noticed that a rather large pile of dishes was in the sink. *I must clean them.* As she was cleaning the dishes, she thought about Nathan's advice to be more inviting. *He's absolutely right. I deserve better than this. I must learn to accept that in order to meet more people, I have to take some risks. Life isn't all comfort and security. And besides, I really am kind of bored. Some action would be great. Get out there and do stuff for yourself, Vlora. Be a rebel! For God's sake, be a rebel!* She began to sway a little bit from exhaustion, and noticed that the dishes were starting to blur. *I hate being tired.*

She looked up through the window above the sink, and saw someone who looked just like the previous night's intruder pressing against it, staring at her through that same black veil. The stranger's hands were covered in black gloves and lifted up, touching the window on each side of its head. It seemed to be getting a very good look at her.

She screamed and dropped the dish she was working on, which then shattered into pieces on the floor. Pure terror grasped her heart. After what seemed like a few seconds, the stranger fled through the front yard and disappeared into the night.

Chapter 4

Vlora stood shocked, and then crumpled down into a corner of the kitchen. She could not think properly. All of a sudden, the kitchen appeared completely different to her. Darker, more disorganized. She felt like she was shrinking into oblivion. After a very long time, she was able to gather up some courage, and called 911.

"Nine one one what's your emergency?" asked the dispatcher.

"There's someone who was intruding on my property."

"Is the intruder still there?"

"I can't see him. He might have left already."

"What's the address?"

"Seven Four Five Nickel Avenue."

"Can I have a description of the intruder?"

"He was wearing a black cloak, he had on a black veil, so I couldn't tell anything from the face."

"Could you tell if the intruder was male or female?"

"No."

"Could you tell the height of this person?"

"I…uh…no, no I couldn't."

"Would you like us to send someone over for help?"

"Yes. Of course."

"We have help on the way, ma'am. Can I have your name, ma'am?"

"Vlora Whitaker."

"Thank you, ma'am."

Vlora's head began to throb. This was the first time she had ever called 911. In the meantime, she remained huddled in her little corner, praying she would be all right. When the police arrived, they searched the perimeter of the house and knocked on her door. She gave them the best description she could give of the shadowy stranger, and let them search the rest of the house. When all was searched, the police let her know that everything looked all right, and that even though they would do their best to be on the lookout for the stranger, based on her description, there was not much they could do to actually find such a person. However, she could call them back whenever she felt like she was being threatened again.

When the police left, she went back to the kitchen and straight to finishing up the dishes. She wanted to cry, but was too stunned. So much had happened in the past hour and a half. She was doing a normal chore, all right, but felt like a completely different woman. *Nothing will ever be the same around here. I'm screwed. I'm clueless! Am I going to die in this place or what? I...can't...think straight. I don't even know what I'm doing, or why I'm doing it. I'm absolutely clueless. What...where am I?* Her hands shook uncontrollably. She dropped a glass, which then shattered in the sink. And then she screamed, for no other reason than feeling like a complete failure.

"I can't even clean these dishes right!" She began to sob nonstop. "What is wrong with me?!"

She went to the same corner of the kitchen she was huddled in before, and there she cried herself to sleep.

****

She awoke the next morning still thinking that her life was entirely normal, and that nothing strange had happened to her the day before. After a few seconds, she realized where she sat, and remembered the disaster of the past night. She then wanted to go back to sleep to avoid having to deal with the new monstrosities of her life. But she knew better. Safety was her number one priority now, and that meant staying awake and alert.

The dishes were not done yet. *Why bother finishing them? They're not my main concern.* She decided to skip the cleaning and go straight to breakfast. It was a miserable breakfast indeed. Too many thoughts and not enough flavor.

After she got ready for the day, she went outside to tend the plants in her garden. The garden was small, only about the size of a twin bed, but had plenty of colorful flowers. While watering the plants, she noticed her hands would shake every now and then. The brightness of the flowers was not enough to make her feel any better.

At about noon, Mrs. Clark called her.

"Vlora, why don't we go out for dinner tonight?"

"Oh, Jenny, I wish I could, but I'm just too busy."

"With what?"

"Well, you know…stuff. Business matters, you know."

A few moments later, Mrs. Clark replied "I understand. But don't work too hard, honey. That could be bad for you."

"I know, I know. But duty calls!"

"Well, enjoy your day!"

"You too!"

When Vlora hung up, she felt the greatest guilt. *But this time it's okay, considering all I've been through lately. We'll still be friends, right? Of course! Silly me.*

She went about doing her normal Sunday activities, which were mostly chores. At about two p.m. she became slightly more worried about the intrusion incident, and decided to call Nathan. *He'll protect me. At least for a little bit.*

"Nathan."

"Oh, hi Vlora! What's up?"

"Nathan…it's not good."

"What? What happened?"

"Last night someone came and trespassed onto my

property."

Nathan paused, and then said "Vlora...is everything all right? Did you call the cops? Is everything okay?"

"Yes, I called the cops, like I wouldn't." *Oh no, I was way too rude there.* "Sorry, I didn't mean to be offensive."

"No! It's good you called the cops. What did they do? Did they find the guy?"

"No. But they did say everything looked all right. The bastard was gone before they even got here. Nathan, this person, this trespasser...it was the same person I saw walking around my room the night before."

"What?" His voice was loud. "I thought you said that was a hallucination!"

"I know. I thought so too...you know what? I'm not quite sure of anything right now. It could have been a hallucination...I mean, the night before last night could have been a hallucination, but not last night, that one really happened...or...maybe that was a hallucination too? I don't know, Nathan! I don't know!"

"Calm down, everything's gonna be okay. Do you want me to come over there and stay for a while? 'Cause I can do that."

"Yes, by all means, please come."

"Okay, I'll be there in a jiffy."

Vlora calmed down for a bit and waited for her brother. She passed the time watching some T.V.. *I love him so much. I can't believe he cares this much for me.* When she heard the doorbell ring, she swiftly got up and ran to the door. She let Nathan in. *Thank God it's just him.*

"Vlora...are you doing okay?"

"Yes, for now."

They both sat down on the living room couch.

"Okay...tell me everything that happened," said Nathan.

"Well, last night I was doing dishes. I looked up through

the window above the sink, and saw him. It was someone, I couldn't even tell if it was male or female, dressed in a black cloak. The face was covered in a black veil; I couldn't tell anything from the face. This person was wearing black gloves, and had on a black hood as well. He was very creepy looking, and was staring right at me. After a few seconds, he just left through the front yard."

"So everything this guy wore was black?"

"Yes. I couldn't even tell the skin color."

"And you said that it was the same person you saw the night before, in your room?"

"He…or she…looked exactly the same, yes."

Nathan stayed quiet for a while. "Holy fuck."

"And I'm not even sure if what I saw last night was a hallucination like the first, or if neither of them were hallucinations, or if one of them was and the other wasn't. I just don't know."

"And the police said everything looked all right?"

"Yes. They found nothing suspicious at all. They said I could call back if I found someone intruding again."

Nathan lowered his eyebrows. "Well, it just sounds weird to me. No fingerprints were found?"

"No! The guy was wearing gloves. There's no way fingerprints could have been found." She slowly said "I could have been imagining the whole thing too, you know."

"Now hold on a second. What makes you think you could have been imagining it?"

She squirmed with discomfort. "Well…I was very sleepy right before I saw this person. My mind could have been messing with me, you know."

"Well, I don't think you should be treating this incident as a hallucination. If you saw someone, you saw someone. You need to defend yourself, Sis. Or if you want, you can stay with me the next couple of weeks…"

"No, no, no. Don't be ridiculous." *Shit! I did it again. I was too rude.* "I mean, thanks for your offer…but it just won't do. I have to be strong, Nathan."

He gazed at her as if she were about to marry someone he could not trust. "I don't care if you think you're stronger by yourself; in this case it doesn't matter. I want you to be safe. Nothing more, nothing less." A long silence. He then asked "were there any differences between this incident and the one from the night before? I mean, differences that would imply this incident…to not be a hallucination? Do you understand?"

She thought for a moment. "In the first incident, I could not move for the longest time. That was probably the result of sleep paralysis, a characteristic of hypnagogic hallucinations. This time, I…I…oh gosh, I'm not even sure if I moved while I was seeing him!"

"You don't remember?"

"I…uh, may have screamed, but that could have been in my head only. I think I moved. But I really don't remember."

He sighed. "Vlora…do you feel safe here? Are you really sure you want to be by yourself?"

"Yes, I can handle this."

Again, he sighed. "Well, I don't know what else to say to you." He glanced around the living room, and then at the floor.

"I'll be fine. Please trust me."

He slowly looked at her. "Of course I trust you. I know how strong you are."

After a few seconds, they both burst out laughing.

"You were always such a sore loser!" she exclaimed.

"No I wasn't! You lie! You cheated in those arm wrestles, admit it!"

"I did not! Ugh, you haven't changed at all!" She laughed, paused, and then whispered "so…why don't we have a try?"

Nathan reluctantly gave in. "Oh, all right."

So they arm wrestled, and it did not take much time for Vlora to win the match.

"There! Now you know I didn't cheat!" she shouted.

"You have quite an arm," Nathan admitted.

They sat in the couch and talked about their younger days.

When an hour passed, Nathan decided it was time to leave. "I want you to give me a call whenever you think you need help, Sis. And don't be afraid to come visit me! Sometimes me and Linda feel like we need more company, anyway."

"All right. I'll be seeing you."

****

When Nathan left, it was already close to six p.m.. Vlora paced around the living room, made herself dinner, and was finally able to finish cleaning the dishes. When they were all put away, she looked at the window above the sink. There didn't seem to be any sign of hand prints or fingerprints on it.

She sat at the computer and began checking her e-mail. One of the messages' subject lines read 'Vlora, Are You Looking For Love?' She saw that it was an ad, but was reminded of Pete.

Even though she had been a reserved little girl, whenever she formed a crush on one of the boys in her classes, she wrote secret love letters to him and placed them inside his desk. She always hid her face when she saw him smiling to himself while reading the letters. As an adolescent, she usually had lustful feelings for the shy, quiet guys. But she had never gone out with anyone until college. And by then, she was so introverted, she simply could not take more than a few days of seeing someone. She believed her sense of pride also had a lot to do with this. Now as a grown woman, she felt desperate most of the time. Desperate for anything. A man to compliment her dark style. Kiss her. Fuck her.

But she was always too scared that she would end up failing a possible romance. Then it would be all her fault, and her confidence would suffer a huge setback. That was more unacceptable than anything to her.

While she continued to check her e-mail, she remembered having lately seen a few ads on the internet for a local psychic fortune teller. Even though she tried to rub the initial feeling off, she could not help but think, *I can ask her about my love life.* She twisted her eyebrows. *Maybe not, Vlora.* But as she thought more about it, she concluded that she had nothing to lose in seeing that fortune teller. *It'll be an interesting experience.*

She printed out the directions to see Madam Susan, and began her drive. It was now night. Almost thirty minutes passed, and she still had not reached her destination. The streets were completely empty. Old, abandoned buildings stood at every corner. When she arrived, she saw that Madam Susan's business was in a tall, worn down, and grayish building. A neon sign flashing the words 'Madam Susan: Psychic Fortune Teller' and the outlined icon of a fortune teller hung above the entrance. Feeling her chest pulsate, she got out of the car and walked into the building.

She made her way through a long, mazelike hallway that had just a few flickering lights. Almost a full minute went by, and she had still not passed a single door. In one section of the hallway, she noticed an army of maggots feasting on a dead rat. She gasped and flinched, but kept on walking.

As she progressed farther into the hallway, she could make out the sound of screaming. The screams amplified until she finally reached the end, which was a doorless room glowing red, with five strands of beads hanging at the entrance. She gulped and walked into the room.

The first thing she noticed was a T.V. portraying slasher violence with the volume turned way up. A wrinkly woman with black frizzy hair poking out from beneath her bandana was sitting on a couch, watching the T.V.. Around the room were shelves stocked full with dark vases, hourglasses, and various figurines.

"May I help you?" asked the woman in the couch,

lowering the T.V.'s volume.

Vlora answered "yes. I'm here to see Madam Susan for a reading."

"All right. That's me." Madam Susan rose from the couch.

"I couldn't help but notice, those screams on T.V. are loud enough to hear from way out."

"You don't like it?"

Vlora was too stunned to say anything.

"Most people find horror disturbing. I think horror's beautiful." Madam Susan stared into Vlora's eyes, then began walking over to the other side of the room. "Come here, honey."

Vlora followed her to a separate, darker area within the room. They sat at a small table carrying a crystal ball and illustrated cards.

"What can I do for you?"

"I just have one question to ask…that involves looking into my future."

"That'll be seven dollars."

Vlora paid, covering her face with her palm.

"What is your question, darling?"

A long pause. "It's simple, really. I just want to know…will I ever have a lover?"

The lights in the room dimmed, and the crystal ball began to glow with scattering plasma-like branches. "Look into the crystal ball."

Shaking, she obeyed. The branches moved faster, and then slowly dimmed. An embellished ankh appeared and began to pulsate.

"Do you see the ankh?"

"Yes."

The ankh gradually disappeared, and the moving branches returned. The lights in the room brightened again, and the crystal ball was now empty.

"The ankh is an ancient Egyptian symbol which represents eternal life," Madam Susan began. She then cocked her head and smiled. "You will…find true love."

Vlora's heart jumped. "But what does eternal life have to do with it?"

"He's here. Your lover's here with us, right now."

"Excuse me?"

Madam Susan's smile disappeared. "You don't see him, standing over there?" Her eyes quickly darted to a corner of the room.

Vlora glanced in that direction, but saw nothing. The screams on T.V. intensified. *This woman is an idiot.* She slowly got up and began to walk away. As she approached the room's entrance, she turned back to Madam Susan.

The fortune teller was still watching her. "Eternal life. Things aren't always as they seem."

Vlora placed her hand on her forehead and walked hurriedly out of the room. The entire time through the hallway, she felt as if someone was following her. *Why the fuck did I do this?* She got back into her car and immediately locked the doors. Without bothering to put on her seat belt, she drove home.

****

As soon as she arrived, she began to frantically pace the living room. *I don't want to die tonight. Why the hell didn't I listen to Nathan? I could have stayed with him.* She walked into her bedroom and closed her window shutters. *And why the hell haven't I closed these in the longest time? I am such an idiot!*

She pulled out one of her favorite books and sat down to read. It was a story about two young people who had fallen in love at first sight. Whenever they wanted to unite for romance, some crazy thing always happened that prevented them from doing so. Their families were completely different. The young man's family never enjoyed going out, meeting with people, and having parties. In contrast, the young woman's family was fun-loving and always made the effort to travel to exciting new places.

Before she knew it, it was time to go to bed. She put on her night gown and brushed her hair. Then, she heard what seemed like the house's front door open and close. Her stomach felt as if it were folding itself into a shroud. *This cannot be happening. I am not tired. I should not be hallucinating.* Soon she realized something had to be done. *Snap out of it, Vlora. Save yourself.*

She cautiously walked out of her room, feeling tiny and weak. Heat pushed against her from all sides, and her head felt like it was swaying. Her mind did not seem to be functioning. If it was, it was in a state she had never before experienced. She began to check her house for any signs of intrusion. So far, nothing. She then heard the sound of water. It was coming from the kitchen. When she walked there, she found the kitchen faucet on. *Dear God, did I leave it on? I don't remember leaving it on!* She started to quiver. She turned off the faucet and quickly marched around the rest of the house, trying to find anything else that could be wrong. Nothing. She reluctantly walked back into her bedroom.

As soon as she picked up her brush, she again heard the front door open and close. Her heart jumped almost outside her body. *No. This can't be happening! Should I call the police? I must check by myself first.* She walked out of her room more urgently than the previous time. The front door was closed. She could not find anything wrong, until the sound of running water emerged. *Please, not the kitchen faucet.* It was the kitchen faucet. Someone had turned it on again.

"Who's in here?!" she yelled.

No reply.

She turned the faucet off. *I need a knife. I can't believe I'm about to do this, but I have to do it. I'll show the bastard who's boss.* She grabbed the nearest knife, and with keen determination and astuteness, she searched her home for the trespasser. Everything she saw seemed to be threatening her. The dining room table looked like it was about to eat her, the garage appeared to be dimmer than usual, the front door seemed to be slightly bending inward, the living room couch appeared to be frowning at her, the blank T.V. seemed peculiarly alert, her bathroom sink looked more like a pit of doom, and her bed looked more like a coffin. However, she could not find any concrete evidence of a trespasser.

Confused, she gave up the search and put the knife away. *I know I did not turn on that faucet…either time. But no one else could have done it; I searched, and there was no one. That brings up the only possible explanation: my mind is messing with me. As usual.* She yawned, looked at the grandfather clock, and noticed that it was beginning to blur. *Yeah, it's definitely my mind. Look how tired I am!* She immediately lay down on her bed, not even bothering to turn off any of the house's lights. Nevertheless, her eyes remained wide open.

After a while, she became bored and decided to read the book about two young lovers. She sat up in bed and started to read from it. *I know I'm past this part. Why was my bookmark still here?* Suddenly, from the corner of her eye, she noticed five black dots spanning the length of a hand appear on the wall above her pillow. They slowly extended downwards, becoming lines. The lines stopped stretching a few inches from the top of her bed. They had been placed upon the wall as if someone with unusually sharp finger nails had scraped them downwards along it. There was no one standing or sitting in front of the wall. *The wall is definitely not peeling.* She turned and looked at the marks. They looked exactly like scratch or scrape marks. When she placed her hand upon them, she gasped. *I can't believe how deep they are.*

Meanwhile, five more marks just like the first were being placed on the wall opposite her bed. She turned around, saw them, and cringed.

"No! This can't be happening!"

Again she heard what seemed like the house's front door open and close. She ran across her bedroom, but before she was able to come out of it, the bedroom door slammed shut. She tried opening it, but for some reason, it stayed shut. Panic filled her heart. She desperately continued to try opening it.

"Let me out!" she exclaimed.

All of a sudden, with a loud bang, five marks just like the others, only five times bigger, appeared on the bedroom door. She jumped and screamed, startled by the bang and resulting marks. With her hand on her heart, she stumbled backwards and sat down on the floor, supporting herself against the dresser. As the giant marks continued to stretch downwards along the door, an eerie white light filled the gaps left by them. It was almost as if that light came from another world. Its rays poked menacingly into the room.

Her jaw dropped. She was absolutely petrified. The marks finally stopped stretching. Breathing heavily, she glanced away from the door and toward her bed. *No. I can't be seeing this.* There, on her bed, lay herself. *Why am I seeing this? Why am I outside of my body?* She then noticed that the eyes of the Vlora in bed were open.

She ran to herself and tried to push down on the body in order to wake herself up. However, her hands went straight through it. It was almost like it was not even there. *Shit! Oh, God...what can I do?* She desperately continued to try pushing down, but her hands kept going through the body. On the verge of sobbing, she quickly turned around to see if anything else was wrong. She screamed.

There, a few paces in front of her, stood the same fiend she saw the previous two nights. It stood still for a little while, but then slowly began walking toward her. *Now this may be all a dream, but I want to get the hell out of it.* She called out to her body "please wake up, Vlora! Wake up!" But the body in bed would not move, and it certainly was not tangible. *If this is all a dream, why in God's name do I still feel very awake? Is it normal to be this scared in a dream?*

She then noticed that the fiend was taking off its gloves, revealing mold-covered, skeletal hands. Deeply alarmed by this sight, she could not help but scream again. As the fiend walked closer to her, it slowly extended its right hand toward her. Terrified, she cried out to her body louder and louder. Before long, the fiend was right next to her.

She woke up screaming. For a little while, she still felt like she was in immediate danger of being harmed by the intruder, but then recognized that the strange nightmare seemed to be over. As she glanced around her room, she could find no signs of a trespasser. The wall above her pillow was clean. The wall opposite her bed was clean. *Please, let my door be untouched as well.* She climbed out of bed and prepared for the worst. Surprisingly, the door was just as clean as her walls. She trembled as she remembered how real the nightmare she just had seemed.

My horrible, horrible mind. Dragging me to a place of fear and helplessness. Thank goodness I have control over my mind now. I will not call the police. I don't need to. Just as she was about to go back to her bed, she heard the sound of running water. She felt her heart jump. *That can't be…it just can't be…I had already turned it off…why am I hearing this? No, this can't be happening…I already snapped out of my delusion! Right?*

She hesitantly walked out of her bedroom and toward the kitchen. *Lately my mind has been leading me astray. Thus, if I see the kitchen faucet on, that would just mean I left it on by accident…right?*

It was on. And she could not help but shudder.

Chapter 5

The next day, Vlora sat at her cubicle captivated by the amount of work she had to do. She was not thinking about the past weekend, because she completely believed that her nightmarish experiences were all in her head. Her clients needed her help, and she intended to focus one hundred percent on their needs, not her own.

Mrs. Clark sneakily approached her, and then touched her softly on the shoulder. Vlora jerked and gasped.

"Now there's no need to scare me like that, Jenny!"

"Oh, I'm sorry. I didn't mean to scare you." Mrs. Clark pouted.

"That's okay."

"Vlora, have you talked with him?"

"Who, Pete?"

"Yes, Pete!"

"Oh, yes. You were right. He's very sweet."

Mrs. Clark gasped and squirmed around. "Okay…is that all you have to tell me? Come on, give me the nitty-gritty! Did you ask him out? Did he ask you out?"

"I…asked him out." She paused. "Are you proud of me?"

Mrs. Clark quickly glanced around the office, and replied "give me a high five."

She sighed, and reluctantly gave her the high five.

"Honey, yes, I'm proud of you. It's about time you

started putting yourself out there more. And so what did he say?"

"He agreed to have dinner with me at Carrie's..." Vlora noticed Mrs. Clark's beaming expression. "And so we ate there for dinner."

"Go on, what did you guys talk about?"

"It was purely business...for the first thirty minutes. And then we started to talk about our families."

"Oh, that's wonderful. Well, honey, I am so proud of you." After a little while, Mrs. Clark continued. "Did he look interested?"

"In what?"

"In you, silly!"

Vlora was embarrassed. "I...uh...didn't really notice that, no."

Mrs. Clark sighed. "Do you want to keep after him?"

"Jenny! Now that's not right."

"What? You do what you want to do, you aren't stalking anybody!"

"Well, he did say he wouldn't mind meeting with me again. It's just...and don't get me wrong, I'm head over heels attracted to him...I think I might be too shy to try to venture any further."

Mrs. Clark frowned at her. "Now, you know better, Vlora..."

"Are you two working hard?" asked Mr. Stephens, an accountant and overseer for their office.

"Yes, sir!" answered Mrs. Clark, smiling at him. "Just discussing ways to improve client relations."

"All right. Keep at it." Mr. Stephens walked away.

When he was gone from sight, Vlora began to fidget. "I suppose I could try," she mumbled.

"You better try!" responded Mrs. Clark.

She bit her lip and said "well, thanks, Jenny, for all the advice."

Mrs. Clark picked herself up and patted her on the shoulder. "No problem. Just remember, there's nothing wrong with wanting a little fun every now and then."

Vlora fake-smiled as she watched Mrs. Clark leave. *Wow, she really wants me to loosen up! That's just so hard for me to do. But I have to do it. I must be stronger!* She continued to work hard until just before lunch break, when she noticed Pete walk by her cubicle and stop next to her.

"Why hello there, Vlora!"

"Oh, hi, Pete! How is everything?"

"Just fine. And how's everything going for you?"

"Wonderful."

Pete smiled. "Is it all right if we have lunch together today?"

Her heart jumped. "What?" *Oh no! I was way too rude right there!*

"Oh...I was just wondering if it's all right if we have lunch together today?"

She remembered Mrs. Clark's words of wisdom. "Absolutely! Where were you thinking of eating?"

"How does Carrie's sound?"

"I'd love that! Did you want to discuss anything in particular, or..."

"Not really, no. Unless you think we need to discuss something. I just want it to be a casual get-together." Pete laughed.

"Well, suits me just fine!"

"All right. I can walk you down there, if you'd like."

What a gentleman! "Definitely! Let me just put all these files in order here..."

"I hope I'm not interfering with any of your work..."

"No! No, I was already practically done for the morning anyway."

So they left to eat at Carrie's a little bit before her usual lunch time, but she was absolutely okay with it. After all, she was in the company of a gentleman. A hot one, too.

"So, do you like working here?" asked Pete, as they walked toward the café.

"Of course. I'm lucky to have this job. I love it tremendously. How 'bout you?"

"Well, it sure beats the other job I used to have."

"And which job was that?"

"You're not gonna believe it, but I used to work as a bartender at that rinky-dink Charlie's on Eighth Avenue. Gosh, I hated that place. It gave me the creeps."

"You know, I've never been there, but I've heard of it. Apparently the food is great!"

"No, don't believe those reviews. The sandwiches have too much cheese, the meats are always over-cooked, the french fries are dead."

Vlora laughed. "Wow, I guess I'm never eating there!"

When they arrived at Carrie's, they chose to sit in the same place they sat in last time, at the bar.

"I have always loved eating here. The service is excellent," said Vlora.

"Me too. But I come mostly for the food."

She smiled, and nervously tried to think of anything at all she could spend at least thirty minutes discussing with Pete. *Shit! Help me, Pete! Say something!* But Pete was silent for what seemed like a long time as well. *We can't just talk about food!* She then remembered they could discuss what they did the past weekend—except her weekend was...*oh whatever. Just do it.*

"So, did you do anything interesting this past weekend?" Vlora asked.

"I did! There was an art exhibition on Langley Street Saturday, so I decided to go. They had some pretty interesting exhibits. I saw a painting that looked like a woman trying to give birth to herself...there was another painting of an old man with a hat made out of strawberries…"

"So it must have been a surrealism exhibition?"

"Yes! Well, not all of the artwork was that crazy. But a great deal did have surrealistic elements. Did you do anything this past weekend?"

He opened the door; I have to go with this. "You know, speaking of surrealism, I had a very…surreal weekend."

"Really? That's…interesting."

"It was interesting. Interesting and scary. I saw…things." She noticed Pete's lowered eyebrows and stillness, so she clarified. "Awful things."

"I don't want to be impertinent here, but what, exactly, did you see? Don't scare me, though." Pete laughed.

She laughed as well. "It really wasn't that bad. But at the time, it was pretty terrifying to me. Have you ever heard of hypnagogic hallucinations?"

He scratched his chin for a second, and said "no, I haven't."

"Now, you may have trouble sleeping after I explain to you, are you okay with that?"

He slightly shook his head. "Oh, they're that scary!" He then hesitated, but then laughed and said "go right on ahead."

Vlora cleared her throat, and slowly began explaining. "So, there are these things called hypnagogic hallucinations. They happen when you're about to fall asleep. Sometimes you don't know if the things you're seeing are imagined or real." Pete stared with widened eyes. "They also may be accompanied by sleep paralysis. And, of course, your eyes could be open the whole time." She flinched as she remembered what had happened to her. "These hallucinations, Pete, are what I had all weekend long."

His jaw dropped.

"Yeah, I know. Pretty surreal, huh?"

"Yeah…in a really, really creepy way."

They were both silent for some time.

"Vlora, I sure as heck hope that doesn't happen to you again. Do you think it'll happen again?"

"Well...I don't know." She shrugged. "It might happen again. But I guess I'll never know."

"Jeez. Maybe I will have trouble sleeping tonight."

"Oh, I really don't want you to be scared. It's all pretty silly once you wake up again in the morning, knowing your mind was wacked out the night before. And trust me, I'm strong enough to deal with my mind. I've already pretty much gotten over the whole situation." Vlora paused. "I think my eyes are open the whole time...I think, maybe, if they were closed I wouldn't see anything, and everything would be all right."

Again, an awkward silence.

"Please take care of yourself," said Pete.

"Don't mind me. I'm tough," laughed Vlora.

When lunch was over, they both went to their cubicles and worked diligently in their afternoon shifts. Before long, Vlora realized it was time to go home. *What a fast day. It went by almost too quickly.* She gathered up all her belongings, and walked by Mrs. Clark's cubicle to say good night to her.

Driving on the highway to her house, she tried to push away any thoughts of horror and malice, and instead tried to focus on her beautiful lunch with Pete. *He is a darling, the way he looked so worried for me. Not that I need any sympathy. But whatever, it shows he cares.* She noticed she missed the exit. "Damn it! That never happens!" With poise and smart maneuvering, she managed to take the next exit without a problem. As she was driving through the streets toward her home, she thought about Mrs. Clark. *She's almost like a guardian to me. Always helping, always encouraging, never disrespectful. I really should invite her to come over more often.* She saw some type of small, furry animal dash in front of her car. She screamed and jammed on the brake. *Oh God...I don't see it anymore...did I kill it? Oh no!* Her heart pounded forcefully as she resumed her driving. She was not sure if she had killed the animal, but was definitely sure that her little thoughts were distracting her from the road. *Control yourself, Vlora.*

She finally arrived home. The first thing she did was make sure all of her window shutters were closed. She then made herself some coffee, so that she would stay as alert and awake as possible. Quickly, she inspected her home for signs of intrusion. All seemed well. *I am not going to become crazy over this. There is more to my life than just making sure everything is safe. Now, just relax, have dinner, and watch some T.V..*

As she made herself dinner, she thought about her conversation with Pete that day. *An art exhibition. What a nerd! And surreal artwork...well, I would actually kind of enjoy looking at that. It matches the surreal experiences I am having. Let's see...if I were to make a surreal painting, it would be one in which there is a woman trapped inside her own mind.* She shivered. *Oh, what a dreadful, dreadful thought! Why did I even think it? Shame on you, Vlora, for even bringing it up. There really is nothing scarier, you know, than being trapped inside your own mind...such a painting would give me nightmares for the rest of my life!*

Her phone rang. It was Nathan.

"Vlora...how is everything?"

"What? What do you mean?"

Nathan paused for a bit. "I mean, are you doing all right?"

Vlora gulped, ashamed of herself for giving such a disrespectful reply. "I'm sorry. I was rather rude there. Everything is just fine."

"Hey, no need to apologize, Sis! You weren't rude, you just misheard me, that's all. How was your day?"

"Oh! It was wonderful. I had lunch with a really cute guy."

Nathan laughed. "That's great, Vlora! Way to go! What's his name?"

"Pete."

"Wow. And how did you two meet?"

"We're co-workers, believe it or not."

Nathan laughed again. "Now, this lunch, was it a date, or just a little get-together? 'Cause you know, some bosses aren't too comfortable with the idea of employees dating each other."

It was her turn to laugh. "Don't worry, it wasn't a date. We're just…getting to know each other a little more."

"Well that's good."

"It is."

After a few moments of silence, Nathan asked "Vlora…did anything…weird…happen to you last night? You know, did you see anything like what you saw before?"

"Oh!" She fake-laughed. "No. I've come to the conclusion that those things I saw were all in my head."

"Really, Vlora?"

What a bastard! Leave me alone already! "I'm telling the truth. I would never lie to you."

She could hear him sigh over the phone. He then said "I just want you to be safe. That's all."

"Well, I am safe. I'm very safe. I know how to protect myself against my mind."

"Okay, Sis. I just wanted to be sure."

"Thank you. It's nice to hear that."

"No problem. Hey, how 'bout me, you, and Linda get together sometime this week or weekend? How does that sound?"

"Gee, thanks, but…you know, I would love that!"

"Great! When would be good for you?"

"Um…it really doesn't matter…probably just the weekend. Is that all right?"

"Yeah, that sounds great. I'll go ahead and give you a

call sometime later this week to confirm a time."

"Great!"

"I'll talk to you later, Sis."

"Okay, bye."

After they hung up, she went ahead and ate her dinner. As the sun was setting, she could not help but feel as if a noose were tied around her chest and tightening up. *Something's gonna happen tonight. I must be brave and realize that anything strange I see is all just an illusion.* She cleaned and put away the dishes, making sure not to look through the window above the sink. Still feeling a little bit awake, she turned on the T.V. and started watching.

Before she knew it, her eyes began to cross as a result of sleep deprivation. She yawned and her head kept nodding forward. Then she snapped out of it. She turned off the T.V., double checked her entire house, and decided it was time for bed. As soon as her night gown was on and her hair brushed, she looked at the mirror in front of her.

When I was a little girl, I used to daydream about such things... She closed her eyes and remembered one of these daydreams. She was a little girl now, standing alone in an oak tree park. It was the middle of the night. However, she could not see a single star in the sky. The only thing in the sky she could see was a very full moon. This frightened her. She heard a howl in the distance. *Is that a wolf? A werewolf? In this park?* She began to tremble. Being attacked by a wolf or werewolf was the last thing she wanted. She noticed a very pale, black-vested man standing a few paces away from her. His hair was black and slicked back. He was staring straight at her with ravenous eyes. She felt her heart plummet. Before she could say anything, he began to run toward her. He still had not reached her when she noticed that his teeth were…those of a vampire. She screamed and ran in the other direction, praying for some kind of salvation.

Forty years old again, she opened her eyes and gazed

straight into the mirror. *What a strange person you are.* Her reflection stared back at her, and oddly, appeared to morph into the same little girl of her daydreams.

Chapter 6

The night calls out to me. Vlora stretched, turned on her nightstand lamp, and turned off all the other lights. She was exhausted. Only a little nervous, she lay down upon her bed, ready for sleep. *Oh, sleep of romance, wrap me in your arms. Caress me tenderly. Let me feel your warmth and embrace this love.*

Thought after thought enveloped her mind. What she really wanted was the scent of another man next to her. How wonderful that moment would be, when she could finally look into his eyes while tucked within the heat of his embrace.

She always wondered what it would be like to make a man cry. Most likely she would not even feel guilty. Such vulnerability in a man would just be too beautiful to regret.

And then she would try to make him feel better. Hug him. Kiss him. Massage him. But she would not stop there. She would get right to the heart of what she believed was every man's only real desire.

She would make it feel so warm and secure he would never want to leave. And in the peak of passion, all his worries would melt away.

Just daydreams.

She remembered what Madam Susan had said to her: "Eternal life." *The idiot. What would she know about eternal life? And how does that relate to true love?* She turned on her side, grabbed the pillow, and forcefully placed it between her legs.

On the wall to the right of the bedroom's door and next to her bed, she saw a hand's shadow suddenly grasp the edge from outside the door. It stayed there holding onto the wall for what seemed like several seconds. No details of the hand were visible, because the light from the lamp was not strong enough where the hand was. She tried to move her body, but found she could not. *What is happening to me? What has come over my body? It's fear!*

The shadow of the person whose hand was on the wall walked completely into the room. It stopped right in front of her bed. While it was there, it seemed to be staring at her. It stayed there for a few seconds and then began to walk even closer to her. In the light of the lamp, she could see the shadow more clearly. It was the same Grim Reaper-like trespasser from the previous nights.

Terrified at how awake she felt, she sat up in her bed and quivered uncontrollably. "Who are you?" she desperately asked the intruder.

Its only reply was silence.

Slowly but surely, the intruder kept walking closer to her. *I'm awake…this time I know it…right?* She thought about the promise she had earlier made to herself to realize that anything strange she would see would all just be an illusion. However, this intrusion was quickly becoming more realistic than any of the others. *Escape…you must escape, Vlora!*

Soon, the trespasser was standing right next to her. It slowly bent over her, staring at her through its veil of darkness. For the first time, she could feel the heat of its breath. It then pulled out from what could have been its back pocket a large, shiny, and inauspicious knife. Her heart jolted. She screamed loudly, leaped off of her bed, and scrambled out of her bedroom. She did not have any time to think; only subconsciously she knew that she had to escape as quickly as possible. Not bothering to turn around, she made it to the front door. It was locked, just as she had left it. Breathing frantically, she looked for the key, found it, with trembling hands placed it in the keyhole, twisted it, opened the door, left the key where it was, and with bare feet ran out of the house.

****

She ran through her front yard with the desperation of an animal fleeing from its predator. Not once did she look back. Her feet may have been hurting, but she did not notice. She only wanted to get away, get away, get away. Through the street, and in the darkness of the night, she ran. She ran past many houses and other streets until she finally found a street which could lead to safety. The nearest place she was thinking could bring her some form of safety was the neighborhood gas station.

When she arrived at the gas station, she opened the door with weak arms, walked inside, and fell onto the floor. She burst into tears. The cashier, a blonde woman about fifty-five years old, gasped when she saw her, and cried out "oh my gosh!" Seeing the condition she was in, she asked "what's wrong?"

Vlora looked at the cashier with madness. "Please…can I use your phone? It's an emergency."

Hesitating somewhat, the cashier replied "sure, go ahead."

Vlora tried to stand up, but felt a sharp pain in her feet, and flopped back on the floor.

The cashier gasped again, and asked her "do you want me to call nine one one for you?"

"Please do," said Vlora, almost out of breath.

So the cashier dialed 911. Vlora dictated to her that someone had trespassed into her home and tried to kill her, gave her the house's address, provided the trespasser's description, asked her to request the police to come over to the house, and gave her name and telephone number. When the call was complete, the cashier told her that the police were on their way to both her home and the gas station. The cashier then rushed over to her and tried to comfort her as best she could.

****

Vlora sat, shivering under a small blanket, in the Eastside Division police station. A few police officers had picked her up at the gas station and brought her here, while other police officers were conducting an investigation within her home. Some staff members had been kind enough to lend her warm socks, shoes, and coffee. In addition, she was encouraged to read some magazines which sat at a table nearby, but she refused. Now she was staring at the floor, trying to calm her mind down.

A heavyset police officer with a moustache walked over to her. "Ms. Whitaker?" he asked.

"Yes?"

"Could you come to my office for a bit?"

"Certainly."

She got up from where she was sitting and followed the portly man to his office. As she walked in, she noticed it was spacious and well-organized.

"Please, please, have a seat," he told her. "I'm Officer Lewis, it's a pleasure to meet you."

"It's a pleasure to meet you too, sir."

She sat down in front of his desk and waited for him to say something else. As soon as he was settled, he gave her a nice, long stare, and began to speak.

"As you already know, we have sent over several officers to go inspect your house…for any signs, you see…that someone may have intruded. You do realize it's been over three hours since they were sent over, right?"

"No, actually, I don't."

"Oh, my apologies…well, they were over there for three hours straight, taking pictures, inspecting the entrances to your home, trying to collect as much information as they could that would imply a trespass onto your property. They came back here not too long ago with the results. The good news is that no one was found in your home. And this may seem like a shocker, but…Ms. Whitaker, there is no evidence anyone came into your home."

She was shocked. "I'm sorry…what do you mean?"

"The officers that were at your home could not find any evidence…at all…that someone had been trespassing either around or in your home."

Impossible. This can't be right. "Are you sure they checked everything, including the doors?"

"We have the pictures, if you want to see."

"No, I just want a simple answer, did they check the doors?"

"Yes, ma'am. And nothing unusual was found at all."

"They looked for hand prints, fingerprints, everything like that…"

"The only fingerprints found matched yours. Again, we have pictures, if you want to see."

"No…that can't be right. There was someone else in my home, someone who wanted to kill me. I know it."

"Why do you think this person wanted to kill you?"

"He pulled out a knife. Very close to me." She paused for a bit. "My front door…was it open or closed?"

"It was very open, and the key was still in the keyhole, too. But did you not simply leave it like that?"

"I don't know!"

Officer Lewis sighed. "In most cases, it's the homeowner who leaves a door like that."

"But not all. You have to consider that at least one piece of evidence, right?"

"Well, Ms. Whitaker…"

"Call me Vlora."

"Vlora…something like that…we just can't consider evidence. Unless you actually remember closing the door…we have to assume it was you who left it open. Especially because of the fact you ran out of the home. Now, when you were running out, did you check to see if there was a stranger's car parked anywhere near?"

"No. No, I didn't. I was only focused on getting away." *Should I see the pictures? No, don't be silly, he already said no evidence was found. But...I must look at them anyway.* "Can I see the pictures?"

"Sure."

He showed her the pictures. All fifty-two of them. And she could not find within them a single unusual thing.

"Thank you," she finally told him. "They were very good pictures."

"Did you find anything unusual with them?"

She sighed. "No. But I don't quite understand. There has to be some kind of evidence for this. I know there was somebody else there. I just know it." After a few seconds of scratching her head, she said "this trespasser...he was wearing gloves. That might be why no hand or fingerprints were found. But it's still possible he was there...you must admit that...right?"

Officer Lewis squirmed in his seat. "I want you to know that we will do our best to be on the lookout for the stranger..."

"No, I want an answer! Don't you admit that somebody else could have been in my home?"

Still fidgeting, he replied "anything is possible, yes."

But Vlora was still not satisfied. "The news. You must place a drawing of how this guy looked on the news. It might save people."

"And of course, we will do that. But Vlora...based on the lack of evidence found in your home...I'm afraid for the time being we cannot send over any more officers for investigation there. However, I want you to know that whenever you feel like you're being threatened again, you should call us back immediately. This town is no place for trespassers or murderers."

Fuck you. Fuck you. "I understand that...but...there's

nothing else you can do?"

"We will do our best to look for this person. I'm afraid that's all we can do for now."

Vlora remained quiet for a while. *I cannot go back there. It's an evil place. It will always paralyze me. It will always cloud my mind with worries. I deserve better.* "Officer Lewis…I don't want to go back."

"And that's completely understandable. You don't have to go back if you don't want to. However, if you want, we can drop you off there and stay with you for a little bit. Where do you want us to drop you off?"

"Not there." She took a moment to think about her options. "My brother's home would be the safest place for me. Can you drop me off there?"

"Absolutely."

"Thank you." After a slight pause, she continued. "Officer Lewis…I hope you don't think I'm crazy."

"Why would I think that? You're very strong to have done what you did tonight; not a lot of people have those kind of guts."

"No…I mean…I hope you don't think that what I saw tonight…was all in my head. I saw someone. I saw someone. I know I did." *No you don't, Vlora. You can never know for sure. Oh yes I can! But really…I can't. The truth is I can't. Maybe I am crazy.* "But you know…I have had cases where I think that what I'm seeing is real…and it really isn't."

"Happens to me all the time. You're definitely not alone on this one." He scratched his head. "The mind oftentimes has a habit of playing tricks on people. A strange little thing, the mind." He then got up and extended his hand to her. "It was a pleasure, Vlora."

She shook his hand. "Likewise."

It was past three a.m. when they walked out of his office together. She was asked to sit in the same place she had sat in earlier. In the meantime, Officer Lewis began to talk with other officers about the situation. *Maybe I am crazy. Not one piece of evidence. Silly me, trying to act strong when I know I am so wrong. I can't believe I'm sitting here in a police station. Why didn't I try to fight the stranger? Maybe then I would have woken up, and realized that all I was seeing was a hoax. But...wasn't I already awake? I'm pretty sure I was...but I couldn't have been. It was all just in my head, a pathetic dream. I am so strange, having these horrific dreams. But...if I was asleep...or in my hypnagogic state...wouldn't I have fully woken up from that already?* A chill ran down her spine. *Yes, I would have woken up already. And I don't remember waking up. Impossible...the incident couldn't have been real...right?* She was now deeply disturbed that she could not remember waking up after the incident. *This could have devastating consequences. I know now...that what I was seeing...was probably real.*

Soon, she began to feel downright exhausted. She yawned and her head began to sway. *Do not fall asleep; you will see things if you do.* With great effort she managed to stop her head from swaying. After what seemed like a few minutes, she started becoming impatient. *Why are they taking this long?*

Suddenly, she gasped. *Pete.* He was standing against the opposite wall and staring at her with his arms folded. *What...what is he doing standing there...is this real?*

"Pete!" she called out to him. "Hey, Pete!"

Smiling, he stared at her for a few seconds more. He then shook his head and started to walk out of the police station.

"Pete!" she called out again.

But he just kept walking, and finally he was out of the police station.

She could not believe what she had just seen. She got up and walked to a Latin-American policeman named Officer Ramos. He was doing some filing behind the front desk when she asked him "excuse me, did you just see a blond man, kind of tall, walk out of this station?"

He stared at her blankly for a while, and then said "no, ma'am. Did you?"

Confused, she answered "yes. Yes I did."

"Ma'am, I don't think anyone walked out. I usually spot everyone who comes in or out of this station. That's part of my job."

Oh, shit. I may have been imagining it, then. "Well...thank you."

She slowly walked back to her seat, discouraged. *Is anything I'm seeing right now real?* Curious about the time, she glanced over at the clock that hung on the wall to her right. It began to blur. *I'm just sleepy, that's all.*

Finally, Officer Lewis and another policeman walked out of a room and toward Vlora. "Are you ready to be dropped off at your brother's place, Ms. Whitaker?"

"Yes, thank you."

As Vlora, Officer Lewis, and the other policeman drove to Nathan's house, Vlora tried to keep herself awake by looking out the car window at the city lights. However, the only thing keeping her awake was the bickering inside her mind. *The incident at home happened for real. Pete, the clock...those had to have been little hallucinations.* When they arrived, she thanked Officer Lewis and the other policeman again, and they told her to call back if she felt like she was being threatened at any time. The two policemen then drove back to their station.

Nathan, trembling, let her in. "Vlora...what happened? Please tell me."

"It's a long story. I'll tell you later. Where's Linda?"

His eyebrows knit together as he gazed at her. "She's been asleep for a while now. But...are you doing okay? Do you want me to help you with anything?"

"Oh, Nathan. I'm doing just fine." A little bit later, she asked him "is it all right if you come with me to my house for a while?"

"Sure thing, Sis."

Together they went to Vlora's home. She wanted him to keep her company while she packed some of her belongings to take to his house. While she was packing, she told him that she was not sure how long she would have to stay at his house. He then mentioned it did not matter and that her safety was the top priority. When she was done packing, they made sure every entrance was locked and every window shutter closed. They then headed back to his house in separate cars.

It was four thirty a.m. when they arrived. Nathan decided Vlora needed her rest more than anything, so they agreed she should call late to work based on a pretend illness. It was up to her how long she wanted to sleep. She sat down on his living room couch. The softness of the fabric felt like a sweaty, hairy young man, pleading for her to come sleep with him. *Take me away from the shit I'm going through. Give me what I deserve.* She fell asleep with no problem at all.

Chapter 7

Vlora woke up at nine thirty in the morning. *Nearly five hours of sleep. Not bad.* She rubbed her eyes, yawned, and stretched. After walking around the house, she realized that both Nathan and Linda had already left to their jobs. *We are a busy bunch of people, aren't we?* She had a breakfast of cereal while watching the T.V. in their kitchen. Then, she called work, explaining her pretend illness. She quickly groomed herself and got in her car to leave.

When she arrived at the office, Mrs. Clark asked her "is anything wrong, honey?"

"Oh, no. I have a little cold. It's no big deal."

"All right. I hope you feel better."

While walking to her cubicle, Vlora thought to herself. *I really need a break from the shit that's been going on. Which is why I'm gonna ask Pete out to lunch today.* She wondered if he had already gone out to lunch. *Nope. He's still sitting there. I'll ask him right now.* Picking up the pace somewhat, she walked past her cubicle and over to Pete's.

"Why hello, there, Pete."

"Hi Vlora! How's it going?"

"I'm doing great! How are you today?"

"Oh, all right."

"Just all right?" *Was that funny? I wanted that to be funny.* "Pete...I was thinking...is it okay if we have lunch together today?"

"Well, I actually brought a sack lunch to eat here today…"

"Oh, really? Well…"

"But sure! I can definitely have lunch with you! What time were you thinking of leaving?"

"I usually go out to lunch at about eleven thirty, is that okay?"

"Of course!"

"Does Carrie's sound good?"

"You read my mind, I swear to God!" he laughed.

She fake-laughed in response.

When it was eleven thirty, they walked down together to Carrie's. They chose to sit at the bar again.

"It seems fuller than usual here," said Pete.

"I know. That's strange."

After about fifteen minutes, Vlora remembered the past night. She did not want to remember, but could not help it. Pete saw her flinch. "Are you okay?" he asked.

Embarrassed, she answered "what? What are you talking about?" Her gaze lowered. "I'm sorry…I didn't mean to be disrespectful."

"I don't think you were disrespectful. Anyway, I saw you flinch. Did a bug bite you or something?"

I need to tell him, though I may not want to. "Last night I was at the police station, and I thought I saw you there also."

He raised his eyebrows. "Really?" He then paused. "You were at the police station?"

"Yes."

"No, I wasn't there. You probably saw someone who just looked like me."

Vlora stared with despondency. "Yeah, of course it wasn't you. I just…see things, sometimes. Well, you know!"

Pete shook his head as if he was confused. "I don't want to sound interfering…but…why were you at the police station?"

"Well, I tend to go there sometimes. I have an uncle who works there, and I like to pay him visits." *That was clever, Vlora!*

"Really? That's...interesting."

"Yeah...I get that a lot," she fake-smiled.

They quickly switched the topic, and enjoyed the rest of their lunch. When her workday was done, Vlora said bye to both Pete and Mrs. Clark, and walked slower than usual to her car. *Shit. What am I going to say to Linda? I have so much to tell her...so much to tell Nathan, too. Damn. I haven't told either of them very much at all. Shame on me.* She got in her car with a sigh, and thought to herself how difficult life was.

****

Vlora arrived at her brother's home at about five p.m.. The sun was still shining fairly brightly. Linda, Nathan's wife, was already there by the time she arrived. Linda was a kind woman, about Nathan's age, a floral manager, and with long, straight red hair. Like Nathan, she was always willing to help Vlora with difficult matters.

"Vlora! How good to see you!" Linda exclaimed. She then ran to Vlora and gave her a big hug.

"Hi, Linda! How was your day?"

"Oh...my day! It was good. Some gorgeous new flowers arrived—hydrangeas, one of my favorite kinds. You should have seen me, I was so excited." She paused for a little bit. "But...Vlora, I want to know...are you doing all right? Has anything happened?"

Vlora took a deep breath, and explained to her the previous night's dilemma. As she was explaining, Linda nodded her head several times.

"Come, honey, let's sit at the kitchen table," said Linda before Vlora was done with her description.

They walked over to the kitchen table and sat down. Vlora continued her explanation. When she was done, Linda looked at her wide-eyed.

"Oh my goodness. That's not good," Linda replied. "But honey, me and Nathan, we're here for you. You do know that, right?"

"Yes, of course, and I'm so thankful for that."

After a brief silence, Linda asked "why don't we go out in the back yard for a little bit? I have some stuff I want to show you."

They walked out into the back yard, which was actually a garden as large as a tennis court, maintained by Linda. All kinds of colorful flowers were there, as well as white garden statues and stone miniature fountains. The sun, which was close to setting, shone a divine light over all of the plants and flowers. Vlora felt as if she were walking into church, something she did not do often at all. *I can't believe how dirty I feel—I am not worthy of being here. My thoughts are too polluted. I'm certain Jesus would disapprove of them.*

Linda showed her some new plants and the new garden statue with two little children playing together that Nathan had earlier mentioned to her. She smiled, amazed at the hard work Linda had put into her garden. *I wish I had her skills in gardening. What a lovely lifestyle she has.*

"Well, I guess we can go back in now. Nathan should be coming soon," said Linda.

While Linda was walking back to the house, Vlora noticed something strange sitting on the ground of the garden. It was a human skull. She gasped, horrified at what she was seeing.

"Come on now, Vlora!" called Linda.

Vlora quickly turned to look at her, and when she turned back to where the skull was, it was gone. *Shame on you, Vlora. The sun hasn't even set, and already you're seeing things. This is your own Hell you're creating. This is your fault, no one else's.*

They both walked back inside. Nathan was already there, getting ready to make dinner. When he saw Vlora, he stopped what he was doing, and asked her "when were you gonna tell me what's happened with you?"

Linda jumped in. "She's already told me everything, Nathan. I can tell you."

"No, there's no need for that...thanks, though," said Vlora. "I'll tell you, Nathan."

They all sat together at the kitchen table. As the sun was setting, Vlora told Nathan what had happened to her the previous night. When she was done, he began to fidget slightly. "I had an idea, you know, while you were packing all your stuff, that something like that happened. But I wasn't expecting it to be this bad." He gazed intently at her. "Vlora, you can stay however long you want here."

"Yes," agreed Linda.

Vlora was ashamed of herself. "You're so kind to me, both of you."

"And you deserve it, Vlora," Linda said.

"We just want to help you," began Nathan. "So the police were gonna keep looking for this guy?"

"Yes," answered Vlora.

Nathan, after a long silence, asked "Vlora...do you think that it was the same person you saw the other nights?"

"What other nights?" asked Linda.

"Oh, I'm sorry, I forgot to tell you," Vlora apologized. "The three nights before this incident, I had also seen someone trespassing either in or around my property."

"Wait...I thought you said nothing strange happened to you Sunday night," remarked Nathan.

Shit. "Well...at the time I didn't think it was strange. I thought it was all in my head," said Vlora.

"But was it the same person...I mean, last night, the intruder...do you think it was the same person you saw the other nights?" Nathan asked.

"I don't think so...that would be impossible." Vlora did

not want to mention the strange markings she had seen on her walls. "The first three nights, I was pretty much in sleep mode. Those had to have been my hypnagogic hallucinations."

"Your what?" asked Linda.

Vlora and Nathan glanced at each other. "Hypnagogic hallucinations. They're just a fancy term for hallucinations experienced while falling asleep," Vlora clarified. "But...I am just guessing. I'm using common sense. Common sense would tell me that only last night's incident was real. But I suppose you never know."

"What do you mean?" asked Nathan.

"I mean...common sense tells me the first three nights' cases were all in my head. But, I'm just not sure about that," Vlora answered.

"How do you know last night's intrusion really happened?" inquired Nathan.

Vlora was silent for a moment. *Oh, God. Please give me strength.* "I just know."

"How, Vlora?" Nathan persisted.

Vlora gulped, trying to think of an actual good reason. "I...I could feel the heat from this person's breath. And...I don't remember ever snapping out of the incident. If it were a hallucination, I know I would have snapped out of it sooner or later."

Nathan grimaced, and Linda slowly shook her head. "Are you sure, Vlora?" asked Nathan.

I am not going to give in to my mind. Yes, I'm sure. But...am I, really? The truth is... "No. But that doesn't mean I'm less sure about it than I am that I'm in your house right now, sitting at this kitchen table."

Nathan and Linda sat silent.

Wanting to change the subject somewhat, Vlora said "when I was a little girl, I used to be interested in the gloomy and morbid. I used to daydream about such things..." She closed her eyes and remembered one of these daydreams. She was a little girl now, standing in front of a large castle in the middle of the night. The castle was located on a cliff, and resembled a watchful skull. *Who is the princess of that castle? Is it me? Am I the Princess of Darkness? Do I have a Prince of Darkness? The world of darkness is so romantic.* A dragon as black as the night sky and with ferocious red eyes came swooping down close to the earth and blew forth wicked flames. It roared, and Vlora had to cover her ears. Alarmingly, it flew closer to her. She ducked as it passed above her head. It then blew flames upon a nearby forest. She turned and ran away from both the dragon and the castle. A twig-filled path emerged from the dark soil in front of her. She had no idea where this path would take her. Finally, it concluded at a Gothic and mysterious-looking graveyard. There was a tall, black gate guarding the entrance. Curious, she opened that gate and walked into the graveyard. A gust of wind closed the gate before she had a chance to do it herself. She then began to walk through the graveyard. *How interesting. I wonder if any relatives of mine are buried here.* She looked at the graves she was passing, and they all seemed to be warning her against walking any further. *Too bad. I want to see everything that's in this graveyard.* A slight mist began to envelop many of the graves, and the wind started to blow even harder. She then stopped in front of a tall, elaborately constructed mausoleum with a cross on its roof. *Oh, how beautiful.* Suddenly, flashes of lightning began to appear in the sky behind the mausoleum. Wind pushed her hair in her face, but she wiped it back, unafraid of what she might witness. Unexpectedly, the door of the mausoleum slowly began to open, by someone or something she could not see. She bravely stood her ground, squinting to try and notice what could be inside. The wind became even more powerful and the lightning appeared more frequently as the door continued to slowly open. All of a sudden, when the door was halfway open, it slammed open completely. She was still standing outside, and could only make out absolute darkness inside the strange mausoleum…

Vlora, forty years old again, opened her eyes. "Isn't that nice?" she asked Nathan and Linda.

After what seemed like forever, Linda said "wow."

Nathan answered "I think it's more weird than nice."

"Nathan!" Linda shoved him with her elbow.

"No, it is weird. I guess that's the way I am," Vlora said.

"You are not weird. Don't tell yourself that. You're a wonderful, caring, and decent woman," replied Linda.

"Yes, you are," concurred Nathan.

Vlora placed her elbow on the table and her chin in her palm. "You know those hallucinations I sometimes get at night? Well, I think my eyes are open the whole time…I think if they were closed I wouldn't see anything, and everything would be all right."

"Well, why don't you close your eyes then?" Nathan asked.

"Nathan, don't sound so rude," said Linda.

Before Vlora could say anything, Nathan said "Vlora, I think it's a good idea we go to Tuesday evening Mass right now. I think some really nice praying to God will clear your mind and make you feel better."

"Not just you, Vlora," began Linda. "It'll make us feel better."

"There's a Tuesday evening Mass?" asked Vlora.

"Yep. And it starts at seven, so we need to hurry up. We can have dinner afterwards," said Nathan.

****

They all got up from the kitchen table and quickly prepared themselves for Mass. *I haven't gone to Mass in forever. What am I supposed to do again? Kneel, pray, take communion…I'll probably pass on the communion.* After riding in Nathan's car, they proceeded to walk to the tall, Gothic-styled church called Saint Ignatius. It was already nighttime.

"I don't think I've ever been to this church," Vlora commented.

"Isn't it lovely?" asked Linda.

"It sure is."

Inside the church, Vlora was in awe at how exquisite the stained glass windows were. Even though they were a little darkened, she could still see the religious figures, flowery patterns, and gentle animals embedded within them. Many candles were lit at the front of the church, casting a Heavenly glow upon those windows and the congregation. Mystical-looking people in white robes were standing near the back of the church. She knew they did not know her, but could not help but feel as if they were judging her. She then caught a glimpse of the priest, a bearded old man whose mouth was constantly open. A large crucifix hung above the altar. Though Jesus Christ was looking down, He seemed to be smiling. *I hope He loves me. He'd be one of the only people who do.*

They chose to sit in one of the back pews. After sitting down, Vlora looked around the congregation, trying to find familiar faces. No one so far. Suddenly, she noticed an old woman a few pews ahead staring at her. The old woman was heavily wrinkled, and there was something very disturbing about her eyes. *No...they can't be purple...* But they were. They were the deepest purple Vlora had ever seen, and she could feel them burning into her mind. The old woman would not stop staring at her.

Nathan finally caught her attention. "What are you looking at?" he asked.

She turned to look at him. "Oh! Nothing." When she turned back to where the old woman was, she could only see the back of her head.

Other than the old woman's stare, Mass was comforting for Vlora. The sermon was about forgiveness, and she loved how the priest at times became so enthusiastic he would almost leap off the ground. She had passed on the communion, but definitely partaken in the prayers with the utmost resolve. The three of them were now walking back to Nathan's car.

"So, what did you think, Vlora?" asked Linda.

"It was wonderful. That priest is really something."

"I know. He gets so emotional, it's great," said Nathan.

They got in the car and rode back to Nathan's house. When they arrived, it was already almost eight thirty p.m.. Dinner was spaghetti.

"You never fail to amaze me with your cooking, Nathan," Vlora said.

Linda smiled. "And by the way, Vlora, if your boyfriend is able to cook, that is one huge plus."

They all laughed and nodded their heads in agreement. Vlora talked to them about Pete, and how good-looking he was.

"Just remember, it's not what's on the outside that counts," began Nathan. "This guy, if you're interested in him, needs to be a good man. And you know how rare that is."

"Of course," answered Vlora. *But I do need to know more about him. He's still rather a mystery to me.*

When they were finished with dinner, they decided that Vlora should go to sleep as soon as possible, so she could get some much-needed rest. Vlora changed into her night gown in the bathroom upstairs, which was next to the bedroom where she would be sleeping. Before leaving the bathroom, many thoughts filled her head.

She remembered the strange old woman from church. *She was so awful. How could anybody have the heart to stare like that? And her eyes...there was no white where there should have been white. They were completely purple.* She shivered. *Jesus will take care of me. I have no need to fear.* She thought about the trespasser of the previous nights. *He, too, kept on staring at me. Maybe they know something I don't.* She remembered how the trespasser had bent over her, an evil darkness in the light of her lamp. *Will he come to my house again? Will he completely destroy it? Will he come here? And...which of those incidents were real...if any?* Again, she shivered. *Who could that fiend possibly be? Oh...Heaven forbid it be...any of these people...* The faces flashed through her mind. *Jenny, Pete, Nathan, Officer Lewis, Officer Ramos, Linda.* She cringed as she realized the truth.

"It could be any of them," she said to herself, close to tears.

All of a sudden, she heard a knock on the bathroom door. She jumped and gasped.

"Vlora, I need my toothbrush." It was Linda's voice.

But Vlora stood still, chest pounding.

"Vlora, come on now."

Vlora took deep breaths, prayed for her safety, took a hold of Linda's toothbrush, opened the door, and quickly handed over the toothbrush.

"Are you okay, hun?" Linda asked. "You look a little...you know..."

"I'm fine," Vlora lied.

"Okay," said Linda, raising her eyebrows.

Vlora watched as Linda walked down the stairs. *Why does that staircase look so shadowy? And the hallway, too? This house can't be that dark.* She turned off the bathroom light and turned on the bedroom light. *Strange bedroom...telling me to go away. I know better. I will not let my mind take control of me.*

Linda and Nathan walked up the stairs and toward Vlora. "We brought you an extra blanket," said Nathan.

"Thank you."

All three of them walked into the bedroom. "Did you want to sleep here by yourself, Vlora? Or did you want one or both of us to sleep with you here?" asked Linda.

I am not a child. "I'm fine by myself, thanks."

"Vlora...now that I think about it, it's probably better if one of us joins you here," Linda commented.

"If she wants to sleep by herself, she can sleep by herself. She's a grown woman," said Nathan.

"I wasn't talking to you," replied Linda.

"It's okay, Linda, thanks. I'm really fine by myself." After a short silence, Vlora continued. "Is there a nightlight in this room, by any chance?"

"No, honey. But there is a lamp right over here..." Linda walked over to a lamp close by the door, but when she tried turning it on, it would not work. "Oh, shucks."

"That's okay, Linda. I'll be fine."

"If you see anything weird, Sis, just call us, and we'll be up in a jiffy," Nathan said.

"Good night," said Vlora.

Finally, Nathan and Linda were gone. Vlora yawned, stretched, and walked around the room, looking at various trinkets and photos which stood on tables and a dresser. *I'm gonna be okay here...hopefully.* She noticed that there was a high window to the right of the bed, and shuddered. *No one's gonna look through it, don't worry.* When she felt somewhat at ease, she closed the door, turned off the light, and climbed into bed. *Oh, how soft.* Even though she was exhausted, her eyes remained wide open.

Chapter 8

"Nathan, I still think one of us needs to sleep with her. It just doesn't feel right leaving her by herself," Linda said to Nathan, in their bed downstairs.

He shook his head and scowled. "You heard her! She wants to sleep by herself! Why can't you just accept that?"

"Well, I'm not sorry for showing a little bit of concern," she replied.

They turned on the T.V. that was in their bedroom. The news showed a photo of a serial killer who was recently plaguing the city. It was a scruffy old man with beady little eyes and a curled-up mouth.

"He's hideous," said Linda.

"How strange, he's loose out there, at about the same time Vlora's seeing these things," Nathan remarked.

"Oh, don't you dare bring that up in front of her. It'll scare her like anything."

"I won't. I'm not that dumb."

They became sleepier. After the news discussed a story of how a lost dog was found by its family, they started to cuddle together.

Meanwhile, Vlora was still in bed upstairs. And her eyes were very open. *Fuck life fuck everything fuck love fuck me someone kiss me take me away from this damn world of loneliness and despair take me to a place of happiness and no troubles and let me lick your body with passion and caress me and hold me tenderly and feel me and hold me take me away from my mind for just a little bit no forever I want forever let us be together and love each other why can't this happen to me am I shy or what I am shy because of my mind take my goddamn mind away from me please I long to be free I long to be loved someone please love me loving me is getting rid of my mind fuck the mind I want passion I love your body it's so soft and your eyes of fantasy take me in I am swimming in the air of love with castles in clouds and beautiful people everywhere I dance with you true love knows no boundaries I know we are together.*

Five black dots spanning the length of a hand appeared on the door. They extended downwards, becoming lines. They had been placed upon the door as if someone with unusually sharp finger nails had scraped them downwards along it. No one stood in front of the door. *This is normal. It's only a hypnagogic hallucination.* She could hear the sound of a drawer opening. *Just go along with it.* She saw the drawer slam back into the dresser to her right. Soon, all the drawers of that dresser were slamming in and out.

The trinkets and photos she was looking at before began to fall off and float around the dresser and tables in the room. *Okay...this is not a good feeling...let it stop!* When she tried to jerk her body, she found she could not move at all. She was stuck in bed, in the exact same position she was in when she laid down on it. Feeling her heart pounding, she tried to scream. She could, but knew it was not much help when she wanted her entire body to move.

No one was coming to her rescue. The light began turning on and off by itself, and its fixture started to sway menacingly above her body. The lamp by the door began to wobble. It then flew across the room, slamming into the wall beside her. All the broken bits fell to the floor. The dresser also thrust itself to the other side of the room and slammed into the wall next to the door. *I have to snap out of this before I get hurt!*

A chair flew across the room and slammed into the wall beside her, barely missing the bed.

The light stopped turning on and off. It was now dark again. Everything inside the room stopped moving. Before she could become hopeful, she looked in front of her, and gasped with terror. The door was beginning to bend inward, as if there was an angry crowd trying to come in. It then slammed open. There was nothing but complete darkness outside for a while. An eerie silence infected the room. She tried her hardest to move, but still could not.

A man's dark figure stood in the doorway. His eyes blazed purple. She tried to move again, and this time, she could. However, her throbbing heart and confused mind told her she should not move. She remained in bed, sweating and near tears. The man of darkness walked surprisingly quick into the room and toward her. She screamed without deliberation. Still, he kept walking closer. Finally, he knelt down beside her bed, and as quick as he had appeared, vanished.

Almost relieved, she turned in the other direction. There, kneeling right next to her bed, was the dark figure of a woman whose eyes glowed purple. Vlora screamed again. Immediately, the purple-eyed woman disappeared.

Vlora quivered uncontrollably. *Why do I feel like this is not a hallucination? Why do I feel the pain of horror? I should not be feeling any pain at all!* She could not help but begin to think that what she was now witnessing was, in fact, real. *I must save myself before it's too late...why won't Nathan and Linda come up here? I've screamed so many times! Maybe...they're already dead...I must save myself...*

Many dark figures, all with purple eyes, appeared in the doorway. They proceeded to walk into the room and toward her. She was petrified by fear, not sleep paralysis. Like hungry animals wanting to devour their prey, the dark figures not only knelt beside her, but threw their icy arms upon her and slid them across her body. They moaned as if they had just lost loved ones to an accident. *Ghosts*.

One by one, the shadowy figures disappeared. When they were all gone from sight, she felt a gust of wind in the room. In the doorway stood the ghostly and murderous trespasser from the previous four nights. Its veil scrunched up into the shape of a frown. Slowly, it removed its gloves, exposing its hands. As soon as it extended its right hand toward her, she screamed. It then began to walk toward her, and while it did, the room gradually became brighter. She screamed again. When she turned to get out of bed, she noticed that she was not inside the room any longer. Instead, she was in a familiar-looking and misty graveyard. It was now, strangely, daytime.

More frightened of the trespasser than of the graveyard, she decided to run through the graveyard and try to escape the trespasser. As soon as she got out of bed, she could feel the cold, damp earth beneath her bare feet. She ran, not looking back, through the mysterious graveyard. The graves seemed to turn into blurs as she tried to run faster and faster. The mist made it difficult for her to see beyond a short distance.

She became exhausted. While still running, she frantically looked back a couple of times, and saw that the intruder was still following her. Before she knew it, she tripped on something, and fell hard on the earth. An immense pain surged through her body. Suddenly, the intruder took a hold of her. She screamed helplessly, but it quickly covered her mouth. *Slimy, monstrous hand.* It then shook her violently until she completely became quiet. She felt a horrible immobility take control of her body.

Resolutely, the fiend carried her through the graveyard. *What is going to happen to me? Where is he taking me? Will he bury me alive?* She remembered the knife it had in its hand the night before. *Or will he stab me to death? What a shame, dying like this, unable to fight back. Will I be remembered as a coward? Oh, probably! My life, cut way too short!*

She noticed that the trespasser was carrying her toward a familiar-looking mausoleum. When they arrived at the mausoleum, the trespasser opened the creaky door, and they went inside. At first she could only make out absolute darkness, but she soon noticed that many candles were lit. A sewage-like smell permeated throughout the mausoleum. The fiend finally stood her on the floor but remained grasping her shoulders tightly.

On a wide table stood eight photo frames arranged in a line next to each other. The fiend dragged her in front of the first photo. It appeared to be dated from the 1900's, and depicted a well-dressed young boy. She was then dragged in front of the second photo. This one also appeared to be dated from around the same time, and showed an elegant-looking family, including the little boy from the first photo.

She was dragged in front of and forced to see each of the other photos. The third seemed to be from the 1910's, and depicted the same boy from the first two, except now he was a teenager. The fourth showed the same young man sitting on a couch with a very dejected look in his eyes. The fifth presented the same man, a little bit older now, dressed in an agrarian outfit and standing in a meadow. The sixth depicted him standing in some kind of hallway and wearing a tuxedo. His expression in that one was somewhat displeased.

When she saw the seventh photo, she gasped. It showed him, now clearly dead, lying in a coffin. He was wearing a tuxedo just like the one he had worn in the sixth photo. She tried to turn around before arriving at the eighth and final photo, but the fiend placed its hand on her head and twisted it back toward the table. She noticed that the eighth photo frame was set rather far apart from the others. *It's obviously a timeline…these damn photos…I don't want to see what could be in the last photo, I just don't…* But the fiend still dragged her in front of that photo.

"No!" She screamed when she saw it. It showed herself

lying in a coffin with her eyes wide open. *This can't be! I will not die like this! Is this monster trying to tell me my hallucinations are equal to death? I am strong, and I will not die like this! I will not die this young! I will live a good life and die old, with my eyes closed!*

She turned around. And the fiend was no longer there. She quickly glanced toward the entrance of the mausoleum. *It's still open...I can make it out!* She ran across the mausoleum, but before she was able to come out of it, the door slammed shut. She tried opening it, but for some reason, it stayed shut. Panic filled her heart. She desperately continued to try opening it. "Let me out!" she screamed. The door remained shut. She began to sob without control. "Let me out!" she repeated, banging on the door. All to no avail.

She felt as if there was still a living presence inside the mausoleum. Terrified, she turned around to try and see if anyone was there. She did not have much time to do this, because as soon as she turned, the candles that had been lit blew out mysteriously. There was now complete darkness inside the mausoleum.

"Help me! Someone help!" she begged. Again, she started banging on the door and trying to open it. After what seemed like forever, she gave up. *I'm stuck here. I can't believe it. What will happen to me?* Soon, she could hear a heartbeat. *That's mine, right?* The sound of it was progressively becoming louder. It was a strange heartbeat. *It sounds so...exposed, so...defiant...there's something different about that heartbeat...* It was now starting to sound like abnormally heavy books being pounded upon a desk.

She thought she heard a rustle. When she turned toward the direction of the rustle, she screamed louder than she had ever screamed in her life. The trespasser stood in front of her, with its horrifying face finally revealed. A rotting corpse face, with eyes that suddenly became an evil purple. The mouth on that sickening face slowly opened up, as if it was trying to eat her. The face was coming closer to her, and a black slime oozed throughout it.

Vlora's eyes were open as she lay in bed. She quickly flinched, very much in pain. When she finally regained some composure, she glanced around the bedroom. All the furniture was where it was supposed to be. There were no strange markings on the door. Nothing appeared to be wrong. Nevertheless, she burst into tears and screamed for help.

Nathan and Linda heard this screaming. They had been asleep for quite some time now, but as soon as they heard Vlora, they jumped out of their bed and ran up the stairs. "I told you one of us should have slept with her," said Linda, scowling at Nathan. They quickly opened the door of the bedroom where Vlora was in.

"What happened?" asked a trembling Nathan.

Vlora, sobbing heavily, did not and could not reply.

"Oh, sweet pea!" cried Linda. She hurried over to Vlora and gave her a huge hug. "It's all right, honey."

Nathan covered his face with his palm, sat down in a chair, and continued to tremble.

Chapter 9

Vlora and Nathan were sitting together in the living room. It was now close to three a.m.. After spending almost three hours trying to recover from what had happened to her, Vlora was ready to begin talking.

"Vlora, tell me what happened," Nathan said concernedly.

At first, she did not respond.

"I need to know," he persisted.

She wiped away a tear, and cleared her throat. "I...don't...really know."

"It's okay, you can tell me."

She remained quiet for a little while, and then said "I saw things."

"Vlora, what kinds of things did you see?"

She did not answer. Instead, she began quivering.

"It's okay. You're safe now. You need to tell me."

After gathering up some courage, she replied "Nathan. I am not crazy."

"I know you're not." He slowly shook his head. "I just want to know what you saw."

"I didn't just see them, Nathan, I experienced them," she abruptly answered.

"Experienced what?"

Breathing hard, she said "just...horrific...things. I don't want to go into details. But you believe me, right?"

"Of course I do. But I want to know exactly what

happened. Did anybody hurt you?"

She paused for a bit. "Yes."

"Who, Vlora?"

After some deliberation, she responded "someone who I thought was real at the time…but now I know…was just a hallucination." She then broke down into tears.

"It's okay. Aren't you happy that what you saw wasn't real?"

"Experienced, damn it! I didn't just see things, Nathan!" She realized she was being disrespectful, sighed, and then said "I'm sorry, I just…went through so much."

"I want to know what you mean by experienced."

"I could feel things. Smell things. Hear things. I…traveled. I moved. I ran. Oh, you don't understand, Nathan…it was just as realistic as this conversation we're having right now."

His eyes widened. "Well…I'll be glad to tell you that this conversation is very much actually real."

"I know, Nathan," she said, exasperated. "The point is…I didn't just see things."

"Now, you said that…an imaginary somebody…tried to hurt you?"

She gazed upon the floor. "It was the same person I saw prowling around my house these few days."

After a slight pause, he asked "how do you know?"

"The same clothing, the same mannerisms, the same everything. It was the same guy."

"Sis…are you sure that it was the same person?"

How dare you disbelieve me! "You know what, if you can't trust me, I don't know who can."

"Sis, I'm just trying to help you. I just wanted to be sure."

"Well, are you sure now?"

"Apparently, yes."

"No. I want a straight answer."

"Yes, I'm sure now."

"Well then. Now that we both know what I've been seeing these past nights is total bullshit, I think it's time I moved back into my house."

He drew back, as if from shock. "I don't know, Vlora…"

"What I need now is trust. If I can fight my mind, I know you can. Let's just put all this aside, and move on with our lives."

He shook his head. "Vlora, it's too soon…"

"Excuse me! If I want to go back, I will go back! Do you think there's something wrong with that?"

"Just a little while ago, you couldn't speak because you were so scared of what happened. And now I think it's just a little odd you've changed your mind so quickly!"

She frowned at him. "Get over it."

"I want you to be safe, Vlora."

My brother. Always looking out for me. Slowly, she stated "I know. Thank you." Her lips began to slightly quiver.

"It's okay," he said. He reached out for a hug, but she calmly pushed him back.

"No. I need to be strong right now."

He sighed. "When did you want to go back?"

"As soon as possible." Not even she could believe she said that.

He scratched his head. "I think it would be best if you got lots of sleep tonight, Sis, and then call in sick tomorrow. Your rest is very important, and good for the mind."

"Hah! The mind…"

"And I mean that in the best way possible."

She laughed. "Oh, I know that." Suddenly, she remembered something. "I just need to understand…that if I close my eyes when I'm trying to go to sleep…I won't see anything bad, and everything will be okay."

"That's right," he agreed. He then walked over to his bedroom cabinet and pulled out his gun. When he came back to the living room carrying the gun, Vlora gasped. "It's okay, I'm not gonna hurt you," he smiled.

Relieved, she asked him "what do you have it for?"

He then handed the gun to her and said "I want you to keep it."

She was shocked. "No, Nathan, I can't take this…"

"You need it more than I do right now. Take it."

With astonishment in her eyes, she took the gun.

"I want you to protect yourself." He paused, and then continued. "You used to have the best aim in the family when we were little and went hunting."

She remembered perfectly.

"Do you remember that?"

"Yes, of course. And I wasn't that little." She chuckled. "Oh, remember how good those squirrels tasted?"

"Oh yeah," he laughed as well. He looked at her with shimmering eyes. "Well, I think it would be best to go to sleep right now."

"Me too."

He started to head back to his bedroom, but then asked her "where did you want to sleep tonight?"

I'm not going back up. No way. "I really like this couch. And it's close to you guys. I'll just stay here."

"All right, Sis."

They said good night to each other, and went to their resting places. Vlora, so exhausted, fell asleep before she could even think of anything. When she woke up, she felt like she was at home, before any of the nightly terrors had happened. It was only a little while later that she realized she had experienced several horrors throughout the past week and was in Nathan's house. She looked at the time, and was startled to find that it was already ten a.m.. Quickly, she called work and explained that she was sick and would have to miss the day.

"Morning, Sis," shouted Nathan, who was in the kitchen.

The mouth-watering smell of pancakes came traveling through the air. When she walked into the kitchen, she saw Nathan making some.

"You want some pancakes?" he asked.

"Yes, please. Aren't you supposed to be at work?"

"Well, yeah, but I wanted to stay here with you for a bit, before you decide to leave."

It was hard for her to control how thankful she was. "Thank you, Nathan."

"No problem!"

"Did Linda already leave to work?"

"Yeah, a long time ago. She had some cereal."

Together they ate breakfast in the kitchen. Later, Vlora groomed herself. When she was done packing, she was ready to move back into her house.

"Well, I'm gonna be heading out now. Thank you so much for housing me. You've always been an excellent brother," she told Nathan.

He gave her a great, big hug. "I love you, Vlora." When he let go, his eyes were wet. "Please be safe."

Smiling, she told him "I will."

She then got into her car and drove back to her house. While she was driving, she noticed that the clouds were beginning to darken. *The last thing I need right now is rain.* She parked in the driveway. When she got out of the car, she looked at her house. It suddenly appeared to morph into the mausoleum of her hallucination, and then back into itself. *I will not allow my mind to believe that this is a bad place...I will not!* She steadfastly walked into her home.

It looked completely normal. No faucets were on; no markings were on any walls. Nothing was wrong. She began to unpack some of her belongings. *Why do I feel like I'm still in danger?   Is it because I left Nathan and Linda?   Or just the simple fact that I am alone?* She could not help feeling a slight sharpness in her stomach, as if someone were slowly injecting a needle there. *I need someone here with me…as soon as possible. I need people here more often now. Things are never going to be the same.*

Chapter 10

Before long, it was near dinner time. Vlora remembered the pain her hallucinations had brought upon her. And she felt a longing for love.

She remembered the ankh in the crystal ball, and what Madam Susan had said to her about a future lover: "Eternal life. Things aren't always as they seem." Scowling, she paced the living room.

Pete. Oh, sweet Pete. I will call him. How handsome he is. How friendly he is. How...perfect he is. Oh, a nice bedmate indeed. She walked to her kitchen, and felt like drawing something. *My love has to be out there. Drawing will allow me to express myself...once and for all!* In one of the kitchen cabinets was a stack of printer paper. She pulled out one of these papers, as well as some crayons that were lying nearby. *Sex has always been equated with death. I wonder why.* As she began to draw, she whipped out her cell phone and called Pete.

Be my fuck buddy.

"Hello?" said Pete, who was shopping in a grocery store.

An innocent, fuckable voice. "Hi, Pete! How are you doing?" *Let's see...yellow for the hair, peach for the skin...*

"Oh, hey, Vlora! I'm doing fine, just doing some grocery shopping right now."

She laughed out loud at this.

"What's so funny?" he asked.

"Oh, nothing, nothing at all." *And pink for those*

beautiful, succulent lips.

"So...how've you been? I didn't see you at the office today, is everything all right?"

Fuck the office. Fuck me. Fuck me, baby! "Of course everything is all right, silly. What, you think I'm sick or something?"

"Well...no, it's just people usually are sick when they miss work. But anyway, how was your day? Did you do anything special?"

Again, she laughed. "Oh, Pete! Like I would do anything special. Come on, you know me!"

He paused for a moment. "No, not really."

Should I draw him naked? Oh! I'll just leave that for my fantasies. Clothes will be on this picture. "I was wondering, Pete...can you come over to my house for dinner?"

"You know, I was gonna make some chicken salad, but that sounds really good!"

"Wonderful!" *Black for his pants and shoes, blue for his shirt, black for his tie...*

"What time did you want me to be there?"

"How about six thirty?" *I will have some nice sex with Pete. Sex is death. Sex is death...*

"Let's see, six thirty, can I make it..."

The sexy man is a dead man. Thus, these crosses over his eyes...

"Yes, I can! What's your address?"

And a slit throat.

"Vlora, you still there?"

Her drawing was now complete. "Seven Four Five Nickel Avenue. It's close to Danneker High School."

"All right, Vlora. I'll be there. Thank you so much for inviting me."

Wow, he's certainly drenched in blood. "No problem, Pete. I'll be seeing you."

"All right, bye."

After they hung up, she looked closely at the drawing. She suddenly felt like vomiting. "What was I thinking!" Furious at herself, she tore the picture into many bits, and threw them away. "You're fucking crazy!" She buried her face in her hands and breathed heavily. There was a loud clap of thunder. *The last thing I need right now is a goddamn storm.*

She then remembered the gun Nathan had given her. It still had to be loaded. Once it was done so, she looked at it in her hands. *I'm gonna have to practice using this thing again. It's been a good ten years or so. If someone tries to kill me...I'm gonna have to know how to use it. I'll begin practicing tomorrow; today I'm too tired.* She walked over to her largest bedroom drawer. Currently, it was reserved for just her hair brush. That drawer, however, was certainly capable of holding much more than just an innocent brush. She opened it, placed the gun next to the brush, and slowly closed it. A peculiar smile formed on her face. As she was walking out of the bedroom, she decided to leave the light on, because while the sky was darkening, so was the house. For Pete, she wanted the house to look as bright and cozy as possible.

She walked over to the kitchen. *What shall I cook for Mr. Pete? Maybe he would like some soup. But he's a strong man. He deserves a steak as well. I haven't cooked for anyone besides myself in the longest time. Let's hope I don't screw up this one.* Lightning began to form in the sky. The thunder seemed to be getting louder. It started to rain. She pulled out the necessary cooking supplies, and began her work. *I could get used to this, you know. But if I ever marry, I'll refuse to be my husband's bitch. Unless it's in the bed.* Her body tingled as she thought of Pete's possibly hairy chest, thighs, and...so much more. Each hair would be a golden or brown guitar string which she could strum along to the melody of his moaning.

Meanwhile, Pete was driving through the pouring rain

toward her house. The roads were starting to flood, making for some very slow traffic. He squinted at the jagged lightning bolts traveling through the sky. A crash of thunder made him bounce in his seat. "Jeez!" he exclaimed. As the rain kept coming down harder, his windshield wipers sped up to the point where they sounded like a ticking clock. Soon, he could not see past a few feet in front of his car. The water around the car began to resemble a raging river. "Goddamn it!" he yelled, trying to maintain control of the car.

The sky was getting darker. Vlora was about halfway done with cooking. *The soup smells delicious. Oh, fill me, aroma of tenderness. I need some filling up...and not just by this meal. I need his body in mine. Will we fornicate tonight? Don't be naughty, Vlora. You know better. Fuck that, no I don't. I need to feel him, rub him, lick him, suck him...make him mine tonight. He'll be at my mercy. Screaming with orgasmic pleasure. And I won't stop. It needs to be all night long, if not longer.* The image of Jesus Christ's face flashed in her mind. *Would He approve of my fantasies? Hmmm...most definitely not. Why the hell am I thinking such thoughts? I can't control them. But I should try to. It is very difficult. Still, I cannot be sex-obsessed like this. I am not crazy! I must discipline my mind and show it who's boss. Because I am strong.* She remembered her brother's home. *You know what true love is, Vlora. Nathan, Linda...my love for them is true. They have showed nothing but compassion toward me in this time of trouble. I love them so much. I would die for them.*

The mausoleum of her hallucination flashed through her mind. She shivered. *What does it feel like...dying? I've always wanted to know. Is it painful? Is it scary? What would I do if I were locked in a coffin while still alive? Before suffocating to death, I would probably have a panic attack. What a horrible death. I can already feel my heart beating too much, as if I'm actually in that coffin.* As she began to slice the steak, an explosion of thunder made her jump. Her head felt like it was throbbing. *Why do I feel so very close to death? Oh, Lord, please don't let my mind carry me away tonight.*

She glanced at her wristwatch. The digital numbers were erratically changing. She paused her cooking and tried to fix the problem.

The watch could not be controlled. Anxious to find the real time, she looked at the grandfather clock. But it, too, was going haywire.

Shaking her head, she got out her laptop. She just could not believe this was happening at such an important time for her. When the clock appeared on the screen, its numbers were randomly changing as well.

She felt like she was going to cry, but was too fed up and decided to continue cooking. She was determined to maintain control of her mind, even if it seemed like things did not make sense.

Pete was now on Nickel Avenue, trying to spot her address through the meddling rain. "It should be around here, somewhere." He finally found it. After peeking through the car window at it, he commented to himself "wow, nice house."

****

Vlora was nearly done cooking. She smelled the food, and smiled. All of a sudden, she heard her doorbell ring. Somewhat startled, she focused her gaze upon a large knife that sat on the counter in front of her. Then she looked at her wristwatch. The time seemed to be correct, and the numbers were not erratically changing anymore. She slowly walked to her front door, and let Pete in.

"Hi, Vlora!" he exclaimed.

"Hey, how are you doing?" she replied.

"Not too bad, and you?"

"Oh, I'm doing just fine. The food isn't quite done yet, but it will be in about a minute."

He nodded and said "again, thanks so much for having me over."

"No, it's my pleasure!"

She showed him where to hang his umbrella, and walked over to the stove.

"So, what's for dinner?" he asked.

"I made you some potato soup and steak."

"Mmm…my mouth's already watering."

She laughed. "That's good. I was hoping you'd be excited."

Several flashes of lightning appeared through the dining room window. It was already nighttime.

"So, what do you think about this storm we're in?" he asked.

"You know, it's just weird. I don't think it's rained like this in forever."

"Well, I think last week there was one night that was pretty stormy."

"Oh yeah, huh?" She turned off the stove and called out "dinner's ready!" When he approached her, about to serve himself, she told him "oh, go ahead and sit down at that table over there. I'll serve you."

"Thank you."

She brought over his dish first, and then hers. They began to eat. "It wasn't this bad during the day, was it?"

"No, it wasn't. It was just cloudy. But when I was driving to your house, it was getting really bad. I mean, I could hardly see what was in front of me, the rain was coming down so hard."

"Jeez."

"Yeah, I know. I'm lucky I arrived here without crashing."

"So, did anything noteworthy happen at the office today?"

"Noteworthy, like what? Different from the other days?"

"Yeah, just…anything special, that I'd find interesting?"

He shook his head and answered "I can't think of anything."

She laughed. "Well, if you can't think of anything, just make something up."

"Well…"

"Come on, entertain me!"

Laughing, he said "well…your friend Jenny, she got in some big trouble. I caught her sitting at one of the financial representative's cubicles, talking with him about non-work-related issues. So, I told Mr. Stephens…"

She could not help but giggle at this.

"…and he went over there and gave both of them a stern warning."

"Oh! That's wonderful," she smiled.

"You liked it?"

"Of course! I couldn't have done better."

"Now, why don't you make up something as to anything entertaining that might have happened to you today?"

I knew this was coming! "Let's see…well…I…how's the food, by the way?"

"The food's delicious."

"Thank you. Let's see, I had just finished my daily jog around the neighborhood. As I was coming back to my house, I saw something odd. It was someone, dressed completely in black, looking through my kitchen window. So, I wanted to know what was up. When I went over to him and asked him what he was doing there, he told me 'I am a ghost, and I wanted to see if there was anyone inside so I could suck out his soul…'"

"Now there's no need to be scary like that, Vlora. Especially after you told me about those, those…"

"Hypnagogic hallucinations."

"Exactly. You don't think it's thoughts like those that might be giving you those hallucinations?"

She paused for a bit, and replied "no."

"Anyway, that was pretty entertaining…in a scary way."

Smiling, she said "thank you."

A strong wind began to tug at the house. Pete sipped his soup, and asked her "so what's the secret ingredient?"

"For the soup? Nothing. Just lots of hard work, I suppose."

"There's something about it that's just so soothing and…delectable."

Don't you dare tempt me, Pete. "Why thank you. It's not often that people compliment my cooking, you know."

"Oh really? I find that strange."

She observed his lips as he gobbled down the soup. *They're as smooth as whipped cream.* She then took note of his blue eyes. There was a candle-like shimmer in them. "Do you have any hobbies?"

He wiped his mouth and said "I enjoy playing tennis and basketball with friends. Sometimes I'll take the time to read. But come to think of it, I really need to start reading more often. It's not that I don't enjoy reading, I'm just too busy for it most of the time. If you're asking if I have any, say, unusual hobbies…no, I don't." He laughed. "What about you, what are your hobbies?"

"I enjoy reading. I like to garden as well. Exercise, too."

When he started cutting his steak, she caught a glimpse of the knife he was using. It was not the knife she had given him. And it looked eerily familiar. She suddenly felt sick to her stomach. *The trespasser's knife.*

His eyes gradually focused on her. "Are you okay, Vlora?"

Am I or am I not hallucinating? My life may be at stake here. There's nothing wrong with asking. "Where'd ya get that knife?"

He lowered his eyebrows and answered "oh…this knife. I've always had it. It cuts meat better than most other knives."

She felt dizzy. *This can't be a dream. No...it's not a dream. I know how absurd reality is.* Slowly, she stood up. "I need to use the bathroom. I'll be back." Keeping watch over him through the corner of her eye, she began to walk away.

For a little while, he stayed still, staring at her. Then, he quickly got up with his knife in his hand and proceeded to chase her.

No! No! Terrified to the point that her chest hurt, she ran through the house toward her bedroom. She dashed inside, opened her drawer, and pulled out her gun. When she turned to face the bedroom door, Pete was standing there, carrying his knife. He looked crazed—a completely different man from the one she thought she was beginning to know.

Laughing hysterically, he shouted "surprise! Betcha didn't know it was me all along!"

"You goddamn son of a bitch."

"What...I thought you were a lonely little soul. In need of someone to hold you, and keep you warm at night."

"Fuck you."

"Oh, don't give me that. You know it's true."

The fire of hatred combined with a paralyzing fear pervaded her entire body.

"I was so close to killing you that night. Now, I can finish the job! You're too shy to kill anyone...and you know it." He smiled.

Dear God, he's right. Feeling her chest heave, she watched as he slowly began to approach her. The morbid smile remained on his face while he was advancing. Little by little, she started backing away. Her hands, still carrying the gun, and mouth were trembling like tree branches in a storm. Meanwhile, the storm outside kept becoming louder and more hostile. There was a sudden flash of lightning, and the lights throughout the house went out. Darkness now inundated the bedroom. And still, she could see Pete's malicious smile. She continued to back away. The image of the candles blowing out inside the mausoleum rushed through her mind. *It's exactly the same!*

She now had little space in her bedroom to back into. There was only the closet. Left with no choice, she backed into it. *I'm going to die. I can feel it. Don't be weak. You fight back. You will fight back.* But for the time being, she remained paralyzed in her closet, unable to discern any sign of Pete from where she was. *Where the fuck is he? Is he not brave enough to show himself right now?*

She felt her sweat literally dripping down her forehead. From the corner of her eye, she could see sinister flashes of lightning outside the closet window. She could not help feeling as if she were still locked inside that mausoleum, waiting for a rescue that would never come. *He's going to appear any minute now. He'll try lunging at me with his knife. But I'll have a nice bullet waiting for him.* After what seemed like forever, there was still no sign of Pete. *I'm gonna have to go back out of the closet.*

She managed to pull herself out of the closet. "Oh my God," she whispered to herself, covering her mouth from shock. Pete was no longer in the bedroom. *He can't be a ghost. There's no such thing. Just like the corpse in the mausoleum…he'll show his nasty little face.* She looked around herself, at the walls, on the floor, on her bed, everywhere inside the bedroom. So far, he could not be distinguished. Even though she began to think that he was outside the room, she did not want to go out—yet. Terror and shock still immobilized her.

"Where the fuck are you!" she screamed. "Show your fucking face!"

There was no reply. The constant flashes of lightning and pounding of the rain did not calm her mind. *Shit. I'm gonna have to go outside my room. And then what? My death? Think positively. I'll get the bastard.* She could feel her heart pounding through her neck. As she was inching her way out of the room, she tried to keep watch over everything. Her trembling became relentless. *I have to be brave.*

She was now outside the room. In front of her was the bathroom. She hurriedly glanced inside it, and found nothing wrong. The wind was now making the house creak loudly. Raising the gun a little bit higher, she walked out of the hallway and into the foyer. It was so dark, at first she had trouble trying to make anything out. Suddenly, she noticed a blur of skin approaching her. Without hesitating, she turned toward the blur, and shot once.

For a while, there seemed to be complete silence everywhere. Gradually, she came to realize that she was breathing heavily. *What just happened?* She was then able to perceive the body of Pete lying on the floor in front of her. *Oh! Disgusting. I must have shot the sorry creature.* Slowly, she began to understand the enormity of the situation. "Oh my God," she said to herself, looking at the gun in her hands above Pete's feet. *I just killed someone. Oh my God.* Despite her astonishment, she knew she had to be sure that he was, in fact, dead. She walked confidently beside his body, aimed the gun straight at his face, and shot once more.

She recoiled at the dreadful sight, and then moaned with disgust. *At least he's dead.* When she saw that her hands were starting to quiver, she laid the gun down on the living room couch. *I'm good, I'm good.* She walked over to the kitchen, washed her hands, poured herself a glass of water, and then drank it. *I actually thought I was in love with that piece of shit. He'll never haunt me again. Serves him right. I hope he's in Hell, where he belongs.*

The rain, thunder, and wind of the storm now sounded comforting, as if they were applauding her accomplishments. After breathing many sighs of relief, she picked up her cell phone, and called 911.

Chapter 11

Very early the next morning, Vlora was sitting in the police station. She had been through a lot the past few hours, and was now exhausted. When she had called 911, she mentioned that she shot and killed Pete in self-defense. The police then arrived at her home, examined Pete's body, and continually asked her questions. Throughout the whole process, she remained calm, self-assured, and cooperative. Soon afterward, several police officers went to Pete's house. There they found overwhelming evidence that he had been planning to murder Vlora. Many of his journal entries, describing the intended murder, were scattered throughout his house in a crazed fashion. The police even found the outfit Vlora had described the trespasser from two nights before as wearing lying on top of his bed. She was then taken to the police station at about two a.m.. Ever since the police came to her home, at least one police officer had to keep watch over her.

She now sat in a waiting area, and even though there was plenty of commotion within the police station, she could not help but immediately fall asleep.

Suddenly, she found herself standing in an ornate, dimly lit, and 1940's-style hallway, in a house she had never been in before. She was amazed at how long this hallway was. Along with several paintings, a few candelabras were hung up on the wall to her left. To her right were five doors. The one nearest to her was ajar, and candlelight streamed out from the room within.

She quickly turned around to see if there was any kind of escape from this strange hallway. Unfortunately, she found that the hallway was closed off where she was, and there was nowhere else to go but either through the hallway or inside the rooms. As soon as she turned back around, she saw a mysterious orb-shaped white light appear outside the door closest to her. This light floated freely and seemed to pulsate with an exotic kind of energy. All of a sudden, the light began to move toward the door. She carefully observed as the light slowly floated into the room.

Incredibly curious, she proceeded to walk with caution into the same room. Inside, the first thing she noticed was that many candles were lit. She then realized that the strange white light which had floated into the room was now nowhere to be found. Many black and white photos were sitting on top of tables scattered throughout the room. She walked over to a few of these photos, and then gasped with horror. *That man! That hideous man!* All of the photos in the room depicted the same man she had seen in the mausoleum's photos. One of the photos was the one which showed him sitting on a couch with a dejected look in his eyes. Another photo showed him sitting at a piano and smiling. A different photo displayed him actually playing a piano. There was also a photo of him standing with two men, all of whom were wearing professional business suits. One photo showed him playing golf, and apparently laughing. The last photo she saw displayed him standing between a woman and a man, all three of whom were smiling and had their arms around each other's shoulders. *Was he really this happy...and normal? He seems so...not that corpse...*

Suddenly, she saw the white light. It slowly floated out of the room. More curious than ever, she walked out into the hallway and followed the light into another room. She was shocked to find that a séance was taking place inside. Everything was dark except for three candles on a table at which six participants were sitting, and the white light which was now hovering at the side of the room. The participants were dressed in 1940's garb and holding hands in a circle. Among them were an old woman with brown hair, an old man with white hair, a young woman with brown hair and rosy cheeks, a man with a moustache, a young blonde woman, and a young man with slicked back brown hair. They were all staring at her with somewhat widened eyes.

"Are you Vlora?" asked the old woman.

Terrified, Vlora answered "yes…yes I am."

"We've been expecting you." The old woman paused for a bit. "Lorenzo's been asking for you. How do you know him?"

A shocked Vlora replied "I'm sorry…but who's Lorenzo?"

"I am. And I only want to speak with Vlora," said a mysterious voice which seemed to only come from the white light.

Everyone became silent in order to listen to Lorenzo.

"Vlora…you are my friend." After a long pause, the voice continued. "I love you, Vlora."

Shaking uncontrollably, Vlora asked "how do you know me?"

"I am he who carried you to the mausoleum and showed you my pictures."

She felt blood rush to her cheeks. Her head began to sway. "What? How dare you say you love me after…" She now felt like crying. "After what you put me through?" Shaking her head, she continued. "How dare you!"

"I was helping you. I was helping you become stronger and more cautious."

She was unmoved.

"It worked well for you in the end, didn't it?"

Looking down with a slight sense of relief, she realized that Lorenzo was right.

"Be nice to Nathan and Linda, because your love for them is true and their love for you is true as well." The voice paused for a while. "And Vlora…thank you for being my friend."

The light continued to throb for a few moments, and then slowly disappeared.

Vlora glanced at the six séance participants and shivered. All of them were frowning at her. Before long, she saw that they seemed to be becoming older. She gasped. In just instants, they withered into what appeared to be corpses. A strange black slime oozed throughout all of their faces. Finally, they crumbled into dust, and their clothes fell flat upon the chairs. The three candles mysteriously blew out.

Horrified, she fled the room. The hallway was now dark. She could hear violent crashes of thunder in the distance. Without delay, she ran out of the hallway and into what seemed to be a large living room. She stopped, frozen with fear. Throughout the living room, tables were flying, chairs were flinging themselves against the walls, lamps were crashing onto the roof, and other furniture items were hurling themselves in all directions. There was no one inside the living room besides herself. Outside the window, she could see flashes of lightning. She then noticed that the front door was on the other side of the room, and gulped. *That's my only hope of getting out of here. I have to run for it and take a chance…I just have to.* After taking a few worried breaths, she dashed for the front door. Luckily, she made it without being hit by anything.

She opened the door, which was unlocked, and stepped outside into the storm. It was not raining, but the sky was dark, the wind fierce, the thunder intense, and the lightning unwelcoming. She squinted into the distance and gasped. Not too far from her was the same graveyard she had been in just a while before. "Lorenzo," she whispered to herself, with a sudden urge to be loved. She ran through the field that lay ahead of her and toward the graveyard. When she arrived at the tall, black gate guarding the entrance of the graveyard, she shivered and felt like fainting. Near tears, she opened the gate and walked into the graveyard. A gust of wind closed the gate before she had a chance to do it herself. She then began to walk through the graveyard.

"Come back to me, Lorenzo," she whimpered. The wind became more powerful as she continued to walk. Dizzy with love, she panted "you comfort me...I need you." Behind her, ruby red roses were suddenly blooming upon several gravestones. "Come back! Come back!" she desperately cried out to the wind. *I walk through this graveyard with courage and determination. It is cold. I am weary.* She felt tears rush to her eyes. *I need to rest. There it is...the beautiful mausoleum. It is a ray of hope in a world of misery and despair. Just a little farther...I am almost there. The lightning races through the sky. The thunder howls with pain. The wind pushes on me, but I will not give up.* She fell onto the steps leading toward the door of the mausoleum. Exhausted, she crawled toward the door. When she tried to open it, she found that it was locked. *But I want Lorenzo...now!* "Come back to me!" she screamed. *A clap of thunder in the distance. Wind goes crazy. Thank goodness I am not. What can I do now but lie in front of this door, waiting for him?* She stayed lying down and breathing heavily. The sky looked dark and haunting. "Please come back!" she moaned. *I want his love. I feel my tears run down my cheeks. I have never felt so alone. There he is.* Lorenzo, now a young man wearing a tuxedo, leaned over and smiled peacefully at her. *My handsome prince. His beautiful black hair, olive skin, and brown eyes. He has come for me.* Sitting up, she smiled back at him. The sky was now no longer dark, but instead hollyhock pink. With the most loving eyes, he kneeled down close to her.

"I love you, Lorenzo."

"I love you too, Vlora."

He reached out his arm and softly ran his hand through

her hair. After inching closer to her, he passionately kissed her. He then gave her a long, warm hug. Gradually, they lay down, held each other tenderly, and closed their eyes with smiles on their faces and love in their hearts.

Vlora was awakened by the sound of someone's voice.

"Excuse me, are you Ms. Whitaker?" asked a female police officer.

Vlora blinked a few times, and answered "yes, ma'am."

"We need to ask you a few questions. If you could follow me, please."

After yawning and stretching, Vlora got up from her seat and followed the officer to another room. There she was interrogated, and a little bit before noon she was told that based on the evidence, no charges would be pressed against her.

At about noon, she met with Officer Lewis in his office.

"I'm sorry we didn't place more trust in you when you came to us before," he told her.

She sternly looked at him, and then glanced down at his desk. "It's okay, Officer."

"I applaud your bravery, Vlora. It's good you defended yourself like that."

She did not respond.

"Well, I'm gonna go ahead and get Officer Ramos in here. I believe he has some new information he wants to share with you." He got up from his desk and walked out of the office to look for Officer Ramos.

For the first time that day, she was left by herself for a little bit. She gazed up at the ceiling. *It makes perfect sense to me now. I should have seen it before, though. So many clues. The trespasser of the first, third, and fifth nights was just a hypnagogic hallucination: Lorenzo. The markings on the walls and doors...they were there at the beginning of each incident. And after each, I was able to snap out of it, in my bed. Now, the trespasser of the second and fourth nights...that was Pete. I never snapped out of those two experiences. And there were no markings on walls or doors for either of them. It just makes sense…those markings couldn't have been made in real life. How foolish I was for believing that all of those experiences were in my head!* A puzzling thought came to her mind. *But Pete…how was he able to find my house when he didn't even know my address?* She shuddered. *There's only one possibility—he followed me there coming back from work.*

Officers Ramos and Lewis emerged in the room. "Vlora! It's great to see you again," said Officer Ramos, extending his hand.

"Pleasure," she replied, shaking his hand.

"Vlora…there's something I need to tell you." He sighed and barely shook his head. "Pete had plans to kill other women as well, not just you. We found evidence of this within his notes. The guy was an absolute creep. It's good you put him away. You're a hero for saving these other women."

Oh, Jesus Christ. "Well…isn't that something?" she managed to utter.

"You should be proud of yourself."

"I am."

"Officer Ramos and I have decided that we have no reason to keep you here any further," said Officer Lewis. "Your house has been thoroughly cleaned, Vlora. There's no more blood, and definitely no more Pete there. So, without further ado, it's up to you now. Did you want to stay here a little while longer, or go back home?"

Relieved, she answered "I'll go back home. I think I'm ready now."

The police allowed her to gather all her belongings and ask any more questions. Then, Officers Lewis and Ramos drove her back to her home. They offered to stay with her for a little bit, but she politely refused. After giving her the key and saying farewell, they drove off into the distance. She walked inside, closed her front door, and sighed. Never had she been through so much chaos.

She walked over to where Pete had lain. The floor was clean now. When she looked at the time, she was surprised to find that it was only two p.m.. *I can still make work.* She quickly collected her files and did not even bother to try to make herself look pretty. After a speedy calling in late to work, she got in her car and drove to her job.

As soon as she arrived in the office, she hurried over to Mrs. Clark. "Jenny. At five, I'm gonna be on the news. Do you want to watch it with me in the eighth floor lounge when you're done?"

Mrs. Clark looked up at her and knitted her eyebrows. "What happened? Did you win the lottery while sick or something?"

"Oh...you'll find out. But did you want to see it with me at five?"

"Uh...sure," Mrs. Clark answered hesitantly.

"All right."

When it was five, they met in the eighth floor lounge. A few other employees were there, some of whom were drinking coffee. The T.V. was already on, and Mrs. Clark convinced the others to put it on the news. After about five minutes of headlines, there was a segment concerning Pete's death and how he had planned to kill Vlora. A complete silence suddenly filled the lounge. Everyone there turned toward Vlora with mouths open. Mrs. Clark, quivering and shaking her head, persuaded her to leave the lounge immediately with her.

They both walked out of the lounge arm in arm. Mrs. Clark began to weep softly.

"Oh, Jenny, please don't. I'm okay, can't you see that?"

"I can't believe it, honey. I just can't believe it." Mrs. Clark pulled out a tissue and blew her nose. "Are you sure you're all right? This was just last night..."

"Jenny, I'm okay. Please understand that." Vlora gave her a long hug.

After a few moments of continued weeping, Mrs. Clark said "it's strange…he seemed so nice."

Vlora calmly looked at her. "It's even stranger how the line between dreams and reality can be so very thin."

Mrs. Clark sniffed. "What do you mean?"

"It's okay," Vlora said. "What matters is that I'm doing just fine, and that you're still my friend."

They then embraced once more, said goodbye for the day, and headed to their homes.

Chapter 12

It was nighttime now. Vlora was in her bedroom, about to go to bed. She closed her window shutters. As she began to brush her hair, she looked at herself in the mirror. Her countenance was like that of a young bride on the way to her honeymoon vacation.

She turned on her nightstand lamp and turned off all the other lights. As she lay down on her bed, she felt proud of herself. *I'm a hero.* She gazed upon the wall opposite her bed. Slowly, she closed her eyes. And she knew everything would be all right.

www.ingramcontent.com/pod-product-compliance
Lightning Source LLC
Chambersburg PA
CBHW031851170626
46807CB00004B/1671